Tyler's Dad:

An ex-science professor looking for a quiet life in the suburbs.
- Can't see how weird Happyville is
- Grows tomatoes
- Lives in fear of the lawn police

Blane:

The quarterback for Happyville High's American football team.
- School heartthrob
- Selfie addict
- Can throw a ball a reeeally long way.

Courtney:

Twice winner of Hairstyle of the Year
- Head cheerleader
- Expert baton twirler
- Rules the school

TO MOLLY, MUCH LOVE, X

OXFORD
UNIVERSITY PRESS

Great Clarendon Street, Oxford OX2 6DP
Oxford University Press is a department of the University of Oxford.
It furthers the University's objective of excellence in research, scholarship,
and education by publishing worldwide. Oxford is a registered trade mark of
Oxford University Press in the UK and in certain other countries

First published 2018

British Library Cataloguing in Publication Data

Data available

ISBN: 978-0-19-276690-8

1 3 5 7 9 10 8 6 4 2

Printed in Great Britain
Paper used in the production of this book is a natural,
recyclable product made from wood grown in sustainable forests.
The manufacturing process conforms to the environmental
regulations of the country of origin.

Graph paper: Alfonso de Tomas/Shutterstock.com

HAPPYVILLE HIGH

GEEK TRAGEDY

TOM McLAUGHLIN

OXFORD
UNIVERSITY PRESS

CHAPTER ONE

TYLER'S VERY TALL BRAIN

'I'd just like to say, for the record. This is a tragedy. **AN. ABSOLUTE. TRAGEDY!** I don't know how to tell you this, but I'm going to have to let you go—you're fired.'

'Well, at least you're finally speaking to me, I suppose I should be thankful for that. But the bad news is you can't fire me, Tyler. I'm your father.'

Drat. I hate it when dads are right—I must

remember to look that up later—I'm pretty sure he's correct but it never hurts to double check. 'Well consider this a verbal warning. I just don't know why we have to move. I was happy in our apartment, I liked living in the city. Don't you want me to be happy?'

'I *do* want you to be happy, that's why I'm doing this!' Dad does one of his 'I know best' smiles.

'Well then *you* move, I'll stay home and get a job.' I grab the paper from the dashboard of the car and flick to the job ads.

'You can't get a job, you're only twelve.'

Again with the 'being right' thing. 'It's probably just as well, there's nothing in here anyway. Where do they normally advertize astronaut jobs?'

'We've been over this, Tyler, I just don't think the big city is a place for someone your age. You need trees and fresh air,' Dad adds.

'How many times, Dad? I can look at trees on Google Earth and I had some fresh air last spring when you insisted on taking me camping—I'm still good thanks. And besides, all my stuff is in the city!'

'All our stuff's coming with us, that's how moving works, Peachy Pie.'

Dad always calls me some sort of variation of peach: Peachy Chops, Peachy Pie, Peachoid, and who can forget the classic, Eachy Peachy Squishy Tallulah Bum Bum Face? It's because I had a fuzzy head like a peach when I was a baby and it stuck.

'I just want you to grow up somewhere nice and make friends, and you know, be . . .'

'Normal?' I ask. 'You were going to say

normal, weren't you?'

'No . . . maybe . . . well, yes. Is that so wrong?' Dad asks.

'It's not wrong to be normal,' I sigh, 'just overrated . . .'

I should probably explain what my dad's talking about. I've always been different. What I'm about to tell you may sound like I'm showing off, but I'm not, it's just the way I am. Like, some kids are really tall but you can't blame them for having long legs, can you? They're not trying to annoy people with normal-sized legs by showing off and reaching things off high shelves are they? It's just the way of the world—the sky's blue, the moon comes out at night, and some people have long legs. Well, my thing is I'm smart. I mean really smart. I'm not trying to boast, I promise, just think of me as having a very tall brain. While the other kids were trying to build towers out of blocks at kindergarten, I was spelling out E=MC². My first word was 'Constantinople' (it's an ancient city that was once the capital of the Roman Empire—it's called Istanbul these days. You should take a look on Google Earth—it's very nice, excellent trees too). Some children wanted ponies when they were little; I asked my parents for a nuclear reactor. Whenever I got a doll for Christmas from an auntie or someone who wanted me to be an 'ordinary girl', I painted a moustache on it, backcombed its hair, popped a white coat on it, and called it Einstein. My room ended up looking like some sort of creepy shrine to the great man, so Dad made me get rid of them all.

When you're smart as a little kid, other kids want to be your friend. They think you'll help them out with an answer at school, it's a survival thing. You surround yourself with whoever you need to get you through the day. It was fine for a while until I realized that they only wanted to be my friend because of what I knew, not who I was. So then I tried keeping my brain to myself—that was a huge mistake. I thought if I just stopped knowing everything, school would get better . . . but keeping smart hidden is a bit like trying not to hiccup,

one way or another it's going to come out.
That's when I started blurting out the answers
in class, and not just the answers but lots of
other stuff I knew too. It was my brain's way of
getting rid of some pent-up knowledge. And
no one wants to hear the answer being yelled
out backwards in Latin, not even the teachers.
I was homeschooled after that by my dad. It's
always been him and me ever since Mum got ill.
I get sad about that sometimes, but Dad knows
what to say to cheer me up. He was a science
professor at the university and he used to bring
me back bits and bobs of old machinery that I
used to fix up. I made a proton laser, electron
microscopes, cryogenic refrigerators, that sort
of thing.

It was a pretty good life until Dad announced we were moving to a town called Happyville, where I get to look at pretty scenery while he grows vegetables and works on his book. I looked it up, and it's this odd little town in the middle of nowhere, which is apparently the happiest town ever. I know that sounds like a joke but it's not; they measured it. Scientists claim to have found the perfect location, a place not too hot and not too cold, with the optimum levels of sunshine to generate perfect levels of human contentment. They've thought of everything—there are three trees for every person living there, to ensure top cheerfulness. The flowers grow straight and neat, and are the sort that don't have any smell

so no one sneezes; the lawns are officially the most peaceful shade of green known to man. All the houses look the same so no one ever gets jealous. From the pictures everyone has perfect hair and they are permanently smiling. I know what you're thinking . . . It sounds like an absolute nightmare.

'Tyler wake up, we're here.'

'What?' I snap. I must have fallen asleep. I get out of the car, blinking the tiredness from my eyes, and look up at our new house. It is big and bathed in a pinkish glow from the disappearing sun. I take a look up and down

the street and each house is exactly the same.
If it wasn't for the fact that they have different
numbers on, you wouldn't be able to tell which
was which. We are number 13 on Pleasant
Road. There's a distant rumble of lawnmowers
as people in pastel slacks trim and preen
their gardens. The sky is big and peppered
with clouds so perfect they look drawn-on. It
feels odd, sterile like a laboratory. I normally
love laboratory conditions, but this place just
doesn't feel right. I get a shiver up my spine
and shake my shoulders trying to get rid of it.
There's an eerie quality to this town, as though
it's trying too hard.

'Let's explore! Look, do you see that? We have a garden.'

'Yes, Dad, I have seen a garden before.' I yawn, still trying to wake up.

'Well look around the back, there's a surprise!' Dad skips with joy as he goes round the side of the house and through the white wooden gate. There at the back of the lawn, glinting in the sunlight, is a trailer. It's

one of those old-fashioned sorts that looks as though it was built in the past by people dreaming of the future.

'Come take a look inside,' Dad says excitedly.

I follow him to the door and open it.

'**MY STUFF!**' I yell. All my gadgets and gizmos are here and a load of new equipment too.

'I got a few things that no one was using from the university before I left. I thought you might like to add them to your collection. This trailer is yours. The old owners didn't want it so I bought it off them—makes for a pretty good den, doesn't it?'

I can't help but beam. Maybe dads aren't

so bad after all. I give him a hug and take it all in. There's a new microscope, some old computers that I could use for parts. There are cables galore, motherboards, and space for my books.

'Oh,' I cry out. 'Does it have—?'

'Wi-Fi? Yes, we're all connected up.' Dad grins.

'Oh Dad, I love you,' I blurt out. 'This is a perfect place to learn. Rather than teaching me in the kitchen—that just makes me hungry— we can use this place . . .'

'Ah yes, I wanted to talk to you about that. I'm not going to be teaching you.'

'Are you hiring a new tutor for me? Really, don't you remember last time? **I HAD TO**

EXPLAIN BASIC LINEAR EQUATIONS TO HER!'

'No Tyler, it's not that. I think it's for the best . . .' He doesn't even have to finish the sentence. Like seeing a train hurtling towards me, I know what he's going to say. I know the words before he does. He twists and turns as he mumbles, '. . . a new place . . . a new start . . . a new school.'

'What?'

'I know it didn't work out last time, but you're older now, things will be different.' He smiles nervously at me.

'You know how school goes for me—I don't belong there!'

'I'm sorry Tyler, but you have to try.' Dad sighs.

'When am I supposed to start?' I do a scowl, I'm pretty excellent at scowling. I practise sometimes in the mirror. Don't tell anyone, but being this good comes with practice.

'Tomorrow.'

'WHAT?' I storm out of the den, the guilt-den, filled with guilt-presents!

'I thought the less time you had to think about it the better. Be brave Tyler—it's all about fitting in and not being . . .'

'**MISFITS IN HAPPYVILLE!**' someone shouts.

I look around trying to figure out where the voice is coming from. A head suddenly pops over the fence. It's a little old lady with a gardening hat and neat little gloves on. She's holding a garden fork.

'Sorry, I didn't mean to startle you. I'm your new neighbour, Jean. I said "Miss Fitz in Happyville". Your dad was telling me all about you the first time he came to look at the house—you must be Miss Tyler Fitz. Welcome to Happyville.' She waves. 'You are Miss Fitz, aren't you?'

'I am,' I say, trying to smile politely.

'Welcome to your new life,' she grins an impossibly wide grin.

CHAPTER TWO

MISS FITZ IN HAPPYVILLE

Is there anything scarier in life than starting a new school? I flag down the school bus and hop aboard. It's like one of those old-fashioned western movies, when the baddy walks into the bar. Everyone turns to stare.

I walk up the aisle, my eyes fixed on the one empty seat. I sit down and put my earphones in, only Bach's Orchestral Suite no. 3 in D major will help at a time like this.

HAPPYVILLE HIGH
The more popular you are, the happier you become!

It isn't long before we arrive at school. I get off the bus and look around. The school sign reads, '**HAPPYVILLE HIGH: THE MORE POPULAR YOU ARE, THE HAPPIER YOU BECOME!**' Eugh! I frown and look at the other students. Each one of them is perfectly tanned and wearing an empty grin, and they are all taking selfies. I hear things like, 'Snapchat me up!' and 'Instagram me later, bro.'

'**GOOD MORNING!**' A tall man is striding

towards me. 'You must be the new student,

Tyler Fitz. I'm Mr Brad Jones, former model and

head teacher.'

I notice that Mr Jones has a magazine tucked under his arm. I can just make out the title: *Which Conditioner?*.

'It's nice to meet you, sir. I was actually just wondering what provisions the school made for after-school activities. I was hoping you might have chess, trigonometry, Latin?' I ask hopefully.

'Why would you want to stay here after school?' he says, looking perplexed. 'There are plenty of other more important things to be getting on with. Maybe get a smoothie? Stop off for a spray tan? Or even treat yourself to a new pair of shoes.' Mr Jones pulls up the hem of his trousers to show off his cowboy boots.

'I've never seen boots made of denim

before,' I say, slightly startled.

'So cool, aren't they?' he grins. 'Have a nice day young lady and remember: **THE MORE POPULAR YOU ARE, THE HAPPIER YOU BECOME!**'.

'I'm in hell,' I sigh as Mr Jones strides away. I'm just about to go through the door, when the ground zooms up to meet . . .

'**MY NOSE!**' I yelp.

'Well if you will get in the way, what am I supposed to do? Avoid you?'

I look up to see a girl with blonde hair and freckles scowling down at me.

'Hey Courtney, did she hurt you?' one of the selfie guys joins in. He's wearing a sports jacket, and a huge gleaming white grin.

'**SHE. BROKE. MY. NAIL!**' the girl cries.

'**CALL THE NURSE! IS THERE A QUALIFIED MANICURIST IN THE HOUSE?**' the guy yells out. Somehow he's still smiling, like his face is stuck that way. '**FOR THE LOVE OF ALL THAT'S PERFECT, SOMEONE AT LEAST BRING ME A NAIL FILE!**'

'Thanks Blane, but I'll be fine. I'll wear a glove or something.'

'I'm fine too by the way,' I say, getting to my feet. I can still hear the laughter from the other kids as they stare.

'It's not my fault you're practically invisible. You wear glasses so you probably can't even see straight,' Courtney snaps.

'I see just fine,' I say, straightening out my

specs. 'It's my first day; I was just about to head inside.'

'New!' Blane says. 'The last new person had like loads of zits, and then Courtney totally caught one. I mean the whole thing was just gross and eventually the kid had to leave.'

'BLANE! DON'T TELL HER ABOUT MY ZIT. I DON'T EVEN KNOW WHO SHE IS!'

'I'm Tyler Fitz,' I mumble. 'And you can't catch spots.'

'First of all, Tyler isn't even a word let alone a name, and second, no one cares,' Courtney snaps. 'Just stay out of my way.'

'You need to learn to fit in if you're going to survive in Happyville. Don't *try* and be an individual, you'll never make it past the first week,' Blane says before putting his sports jacket over Courtney's shoulders and escorting her gently away, 'Come on hon, let's get you a nail file.'

Suddenly I feel very small indeed. I head in towards the office and tap at the window in reception.

'Excuse me? I'm Tyler Fitz.'

'Are you the new girl?' the receptionist asks, her eyes still fixed to her computer screen.

'Yes.'

'Here's the timetable, lunch is at one. Have a good day. And remember—a smile costs nothing!'

I look down at the timetable and the first

lesson is . . . A History of Jeans: the first two hundred years.

'Oh great!' I cry. 'Since when was the history of denim a subject?'

I didn't think this place could get any weirder but then I spent the morning learning the best place to add rips to my jeans. You should have seen the looks on everyone's faces when I told them I don't own a pair. Then it was photography—sounds fun, right? The whole lesson consisted of finding the best filter to use when posting a picture of your skinny latte online.

It's lunchtime now but I can't face the cafeteria

so I decide to go for a walk instead.

At last I find what looks like an empty room. Perhaps I can read my dictionary in here, in peace? It's dark inside and I can hear my heart pounding in my ears—this place feels spooky. I scan the room, looking for a light switch.

'You are experiencing a natural response to the hormone adrenaline,' I whisper to myself. 'This is your body's way of preparing you for perceived danger. It's not real, there's no such thing as monsters or things that go bump in the night.'

BUMP!

I freeze. OK, that was a coincidence. Mustn't scream, even though I appear to be trapped in a bad horror movie.

Slowly my eyes adjust to the dark, and I make out some movement in the far corner. What is this place?

'Yes, I stopped mortals from foreseeing their doom,' a voice booms.

'Hello?' I call out nervously. I sense whispering and scampering of feet. It feels as though I'm being surrounded and then suddenly and without warning, someone flicks on the light switch.

'**STAY BACK, I'M ARMED!**' I yell, closing my eyes against the blinding brightness and waving my hands around with a deadly combination of karate chops.

'Armed with what?' I hear someone ask.

'I'm armed with . . . arms!' I open my eyes
slowly and finally take in where I am. It isn't scary
at all—this is my spiritual home! Some kids have
the mall, others a sports field, I have the library.
And there in front of me are two awkward-looking
girls. They look, well, normal, like me.

'I'm Tyler Fitz, but call me Fitz,' I say. 'Why
were you sitting in the dark?'

'I'm Ashley and this is Dylan,' one of the
girls replies. 'We're kind of ahead in most of our
classes, so they send us out here to the library
so we don't bother the other kids.'

'Some of them throw things at us because
we're clever.' Dylan smiles as if that's normal.

The girl who introduced herself as Ashley has thick square glasses, a cool afro, and is dwarfed by a big rucksack. Dylan is smaller than Ashley and me. She has thick bunches on the side of her head, and a big smile. A really big smile that shows off her braces. Dylan waves maniacally and I wave back.

'No one ever comes in here so we were practising our Greek tragedy. It's more atmospheric with the lights off. I hope we didn't scare you?'

'I was terrified,' I say. 'But I guess that's a good thing, it means you were good. All that stuff about mortals foreseeing their doom. Is it for a school production?'

'No, it's just for us, really. We like to put on a play every spring. No one ever comes except us of course, but it's a lot of fun,' Dylan replies enthusiastically.

'You should have seen my Hamlet,' Ashley says, deadpan. 'I gave myself a standing ovation.'

'*Hamlet*. That's a bit bleak, isn't it?' I ask.

'Art shouldn't be fun, it should be about truth,' Ashley says.

'Lighten up, Ash— she can be a bit serious at times.' Dylan winks at me.

'I see,' and I can't help but smile.

'Why is her face doing that?' Ashley asks. 'Is she laughing at us?'

'No, she's happy,' replies Dylan.

'Sorry,' I say, smiling even more. I'm suddenly overcome with so much happiness that I can't help but hug them—it's awkward hugging, but hugging all the same.

'**NERDS!**' I grin. '**REAL-LIFE BEAUTIFUL NERDS!**' I squeeze them again, tightly, and my glasses fall off and Dylan's watch gets caught in my hair.

'**PERSONAL SPACE ISSUES, PERSONAL SPACE ISSUES!**' Ashley cries. 'Are you going to take our lunch money? 86.3% of all physical contact at school leads to misery.'

'No Ashley, look at her, she's one of us! I think she might be a friend,' Dylan giggles.

'**BUT I CAN'T LOOK AT HER! I CAN'T SEE ANYTHING!**' Ashley wails.

'Try cleaning your glasses, Ashley,' Dylan sighs.

'Sorry, they steam up in times of tension. The internet went down at home last year and I couldn't see for a month,' she says, giving them a wipe on her jumper before placing them carefully back on her face.

'Oh my, can it be true?' Ashley squeals. **'THERE'S ANOTHER ONE OF US! WE HAVE A FRIEND!** You won't leave us, will you? We had a friend once who left for Europe. She said she'd write but we didn't hear a thing. If you're going to let us down, I'd rather know about it now,' says Dylan.

'I'm afraid you're stuck with me,' I laugh and I know at that moment that it's going to be OK. I have found my people. In the library no less!

'Is this your first day?' Dylan asks.

'Yeah, I just moved from the city.'

'Oooh, the city,' they both say excitedly.

'Is it true that you can wear what you want there?' Dylan asks giddily.

'Yep.'

'And is it true they have huge libraries the size of football stadiums?' Ashley asks, her eyes as big as saucers.

'Yep.'

'And people go in them, and people don't throw things at your head?'

'Yep and yep!' I add.

'One day, I'm totally going there,' Dylan chuckles. 'Hey, do you want to come and see our stuff, Fitz?'

'Wait, this is a big step.' Ashley looks at Dylan. 'What if she's not . . .'

'Not what?' I say curiously.

'Not nerd enough,' Dylan sighs. 'This is like Janice all over again.' Dylan glares at Ashley and shakes her head.

'All I'm saying is that to be our friend, there should be some sort of exam, or test. Why is that so bad?' Ashley demands.

'Who's Janice? Is she the friend of yours that went to Europe?' I ask, trying to catch up.

'No, Janice was new to the school, like you. She was nice, her hair had sparkly bits in, and she had a kind face,' Dylan explains.

'She wanted to be our friend, so I asked her a couple of basic questions. I wouldn't say it was an interview as such . . . I asked her where she saw herself in five years' time and what the square root of 34,562 was.'

'She'd only asked to borrow your pencil sharpener!' Dylan says, throwing her arms in the air.

'Lack of preparation is weakness,' Ashley adds darkly.

'So as you can imagine, *she* never spoke to us again.' Dylan looks sad.

'Well, firstly, who uses pencils any more? And secondly, in five years' time I see myself at one of the country's top universities, probably tutoring, and lastly 185.9085796836714,' I reel off.

'Impressive.' Ashley nods respectfully. 'I'd shake your hand but that goes against all my rules with regards to invasions of personal space.'

'I hear that,' I nod.

'Come this way!' Dylan jumps up and down like all the excitement is about to fly out of her.

They lead me between the bookshelves as we snake to the back of the library. It's dark and dusty and it feels as though no one has been down here for decades. A library is like a time machine, it can take you anywhere—forwards, backwards, even to other galaxies, just by picking up a book. But this place looks like it's been abandoned, unloved, and unwanted. It's a crime. Just when I think we're about to come to a dead end, we turn the corner and we come to a dead end. There's just a wall with a vent. Ashley goes over to it, pulls out a screwdriver from her backpack, flips it in the air and catches it again, like a baton. With a few moves of the wrist, the vent's open and she pulls out an old box full of gizmos and gadgets of all kinds. I feel like a kid on Christmas day.

'You've got a quantum sensor and is that a particle accelerator too?' I scream with joy. 'May I?'

'I knew she was one of us,' Dylan smiles. 'Go ahead.'

'Where did you get all this from?' I ask as I start tinkering with buttons and switches, like I'm playing a giant piano.

'Bits that no one uses, bits we find in junk shops, basically anything we can get hold of. We have to hide it because if the other kids knew, they'd break it. They like to break our stuff, ' Dylan says sadly before smiling again and turning to her friend. 'Ashley is the inventor; she can turn any collection of junk into something useful. Computers, robots, you name it—last year she turned a scooter into a flying machine.'

'Wow, really, what happened?' I ask.

'My glasses steamed up and I crashed into a tree,' Ashley says, rubbing her head. 'I never would have made it if Dylan hadn't hacked into NASA to get the design blueprints for their latest jet engines.'

'I like computers,' Dylan shrugs.

'She's a computer genius! She can hack her way through any firewall with her eyes closed.'

'I like candy too. Computers and candy. Do you like candy? I've ranked my favourite candy bars in order; I came up with an algorithm to work out which is best. Maybe you could come over and see my spreadsheet sometime?' Dylan says, shyly. 'What about you, do you have a thing?'

'Well, I can remember things—facts, figures—and once they're in here,' I tap my head, 'they're not going anywhere.'

'Hey, is that an electromagnetic field reader?' I ask. 'I may know a place we can keep all this, because I have "stuff" too,' I say, thinking about the den.

'Oh my goodness, she knows about electromagnetism and she has "stuff" too. I'm so happy! Do you want to come for a sleepover, or even a movie?' Dylan asks. I nod enthusiastically and she stares at me for a moment beaming with joy, then quickly turns to Ashley and punches her straight in the face.

'OW, WHAT DID YOU DO THAT FOR?'
Ashley yelps, falling backwards into a bookcase.

'I was going for a fist bump!' Dylan yells, looking worried.

'Well don't!' Ashley cries out in pain.

Just at that second the bell rings loudly and we all jump out of our skin.

'Oh no, we've got sports next,' Ashley sighs rubbing her nose. 'That means jocks and cheerleaders. They hate us.'

'Shall we hide in the usual place?' Dylan asks. 'There's an extra trash can if you want to join us, Fitz?'

'OK . . . no wait, this isn't right, hiding in a

trash can? We can't keep hiding all the time. Imagine if I'd hidden from you both, I would probably be sat on my own in some dark corner of the library right now. Maybe my dad was right, maybe school is about being brave. Why can't we go out there and just be ourselves?'

'People don't like people who are just themselves!' Ashley sighs. 'But it's not just that—this town is weird. Spooky things that no one can explain happen all the time but it's like we're the only ones who notice. Everyone is so obsessed with keeping this perfect facade that all the weird stuff that happens gets swept under the carpet.'

'That's why we like to keep a low profile,' Dylan adds in a serious voice.

'BY HIDING IN THE TRASH? NO, WE'RE BETTER THAN THAT! Listen, this place can't be *that* weird. Think about it—we're smart enough to take anyone on. Ashley, you are an amazing inventor. Dylan, you're a computer genius and I have an IQ that is out of this world! Together, there's nothing this school or town can throw at us,' I say, triumphantly.

'But I do have an actual phobia of physical sport,' Dylan pleads.

'And I'm allergic to pretty much everything: gluten, lactose, heights . . .' Ashley adds.

'None of that matters—wait, *can* you be allergic to heights?' I interrupt myself.

'Yeah, I puke like a washing machine on the spin cycle if I climb the stairs too quickly.'

'Duly noted,' I continue, 'but we've got brains and now we've got each other! All we have to do is go out into that school, into that town, and stand up for ourselves.'

Dylan pulls out her inhaler and takes a deep puff, and then she twirls it like a cowboy's pistol back into her pocket. I glance over at Ashley who tries to wink—it just looks as though she has something in her eye but I think that means she's in. 'Cool,' I say grinning, **NOW LET'S GET OUR NERD ON!'**

CHAPTER THREE

SCHOOL OF GEEKS

I fling open the library doors and we stride into the corridor. If this were a film, some rousing pop music would be playing in the background and all three of us would be walking in slow motion. We grin at each other as we see everyone's faces. There are gasps; people run away; I even see one or two recoil like they've just seen a hairy spider. I don't think anyone in this town's seen so many nerds together

before. I wonder what the collective noun is.
A flock of nerds . . . hmmm . . . what about a
school of geeks? Probably the latter. I've never
felt cooler, I've never felt more alive, more
proud to be me. Finally after years of being an
outcast, I have done something normal—I have
made friends. And not just any friends, I have

found my tribe and it feels pretty good. OK, so I didn't want to go to school, but maybe this whole thing was meant to be? I would call it fate except that fate doesn't actually exist: it's just a series of random events all interacting with each other, but you know what I mean.

I look either side of me. Ashley is strutting too, her eyes are narrowed and a big smile is painted across her face. People are flinging themselves out of the way. On the other side, Dylan is doing finger pistols at everyone in her way and winking as she goes. Maybe this will be the moment when we rise and take back the world from normals? I am invincible, I am unbreakable! I have absolutely no idea where I'm going . . . it's at that moment I realize that the thing about marching purposefully down a corridor is that you need a destination.

Should I tell the others I have no idea where I'm going? I look around for the sports hall. Why don't any of the doors have labels? Perhaps it doesn't matter, I think hopefully. Perhaps all I need to do is choose a door and it will be the right one? Yes, I should just pick this door and go through it, and on the other side will be a happy future! I grin and open the next door on my left. It's the wrong door. There is no sport in here, only shelves with heavy stuff on. Dylan and Ashley follow me in and before I know what's happened I've fallen over for the second time today. There's a huge clatter as mops, toilet rolls, and buckets come tumbling down on us.

'Why did you lead us in here?' Dylan says,
taking the bucket off her head.

'I didn't know where the sports hall was so
I took a guess. **YOU COULD HAVE TOLD ME
THIS WAS THE JANITOR'S CUPBOARD!**'

'I see you've finally found a career to match

your clothes,' a familiar voice snarks. I turn around and there's Courtney again, looking very pleased with herself. 'Because you know, you dress like a janitor,' she adds.

'Yes, I know, I got it.'

'Because that's what you belong doing—you know, cleaning up poop and stuff,' Courtney says.

'Yes, I got it the first time,' I say, resisting the urge to thwack her with a mop.

'And I see you found the other **FREAKAZOIDS** too,' she says, shaking her head. 'So what, now you guys are hanging out, using big words, and reading books, like that's even a thing any more. And Dylan, where's my money, remember the agreement?'

'Hi Courtney, your money will be in your account by the end of the week as per usual.' Dylan says.

'It better be, skinny soya lattes aren't cheap,' Courtney scoffs.

'What money?' I ask, trying to unravel the toilet roll that's around my head and just getting more caught up.

'Oh, well, Courtney used to steal my dinner money but it was getting a bit tedious so we decided a much better way to do it was via weekly payment on my phone.'

'It takes the admin out of it, I don't do admin,' Courtney says, looking at her broken nail with a scowl.

Dylan nods, looking resigned.

'Smile please, Dylan, you know you can get a note from the teacher for not looking happy? Three frowns and you get suspended. Do you want me to have to tell on you? It's like you hate yourself or something.'

'SMILE? ARE YOU NUTS? YOU'RE BULLYING HER!' I turn to face Dylan, **'SHE'S BULLYING YOU—AND STEALING FROM YOU!'** I yell.

'She *gifts* it to me. Gifting is not stealing. It's like a completely different word. You think you'd know this, being a book lover.'

'I don't care,' I say, grabbing Dylan's phone.

'What are you doing?' Dylan asks.

'Yeah, what are you doing?' Courtney gasps.

'I'm giving Dylan her money back.' I hit the app and with a few tweaks of the settings I cancel the payments.

'**YOU CAN'T DO THAT!**' Courtney shrieks.

'Well she just did,' Ashley smirks.

'She can't, it's my money. It's stealing!'

'Don't think of it as stealing, just re-gifting; it can't be stealing because it's a completely different word,' I say, handing back Dylan's phone. 'Now, when can you pay her back everything that she's given you already?' I say.

'**HA! NICE ONE FITZ!**' Ashley laughs.

'Fitz is it?' Courtney stares at me.

'Tyler Fitz. I told you my name this morning,' I helpfully point out.

'You think you're so clever, with your "remembering things" and your "voice", don't you? Well this isn't over, Fitz. This is the happiest town in the world, and I don't want you and your weird friends spoiling it. Isn't there some rule against more than one nerd gathering in a public place? You have just made an enemy.' She stares at me like she's going to hurt me but can't decide whether roughing me up is going to ruin her hair. Before she can make up her mind, a couple of cheerleaders touch her on the arm and pull her away.

'Come on Courtney, it's the big game, we don't want to be late. Stay away from these "people"; you don't want to catch a spot again, it's homecoming in a month.'

'**YOU CAN'T CATCH SPOTS!**' I yell, but it's too late, they're gone.

'Wow, that was incredible,' Dylan bursts out. 'You totally won. I am free of her, I mean she's going to make my life a misery from now until the day I die, but in *some* ways I'm free of her. Maybe I could use the money I've just saved to hire a bodyguard, or move house or change my name or have plastic surgery so I look different. I've always been a huge fan of Charles Darwin, I wonder if I could get that look. Would I suit an enormous bushy beard?'

'You're babbling, Dylan,' Ashley says, giving her a shake. 'Come on, we're going to be late.'

We all climb out of the cupboard looking like three Egyptian mummies draped in rolls of paper.

'**ARGH ZOMBIES!**' someone yells.

'We're not zombies, we are just three girls draped in toilet rolls. People really are odd in this place, aren't they?' I watch as he runs off screaming. 'What's the deal with Courtney anyway?'

'She's Miss Popular, head cheerleader, captain of the dance team, twice winner of hairstyle of the year. She's like royalty round here,' Ashley tells me.

'You have a vote about hair?' I ask.

'Last year I got the loser's prize and had to wear the "**HAT OF SHAME**" for three weeks,'

Dylan says, shrugging her shoulders. 'But I love hats, so the joke's on them!' she grins. 'Come on, the gym's this way.' Dylan pulls me up.

'What do we do in sports anyway?' I ask, as we walk towards the sports hall, for real this time. 'I hope you have a bridge club. Some people don't think of bridge as a sport, but it's so much more than a card game. I once sweated a great deal during a very tense game, that's the definition of sport isn't it, sweating?' I ask.

'I don't think so, my dad sweats whenever he eats a big pork chop. I'm pretty sure that hasn't made the Olympics yet,' Ashley replies, holding a door open which says Sports Hall.

'WELCOME TO CHEERLEADING CLASS!'

Ashley smiles sarcastically as I peer inside.

First I'm dazzled by the whiteness of the teeth,

then by the smell of the hairspray—it's so

sweet and sickly and so powerful that I can't

help but . . . **THUD!**

CHAPTER FOUR

A RAINBOW MADE OF SCREAMS

I wake feeling very woozy. There's a lady looking into my eyes waving a tiny torch.

'CAN YOU HEAR ME? HOW MANY FINGERS AM I HOLDING UP?'

'FOUR!' I yell back. **'WHAT ARE WE DOING?'**

'I'M THE NURSE, CAN YOU SMILE FOR ME?'

'I DON'T REALLY FEEL LIKE IT, MY HEAD IS QUITE PAINFUL.' I blink my eyes and the world comes into focus. I see Ashley and Dylan looking at me closely.

The nurse turns to them and shakes her head. 'She seems fine, but I'm worried by the lack of smiling.'

'A head injury will do that to some people.' Ashley shrugs.

'What happened, did she get hit by a flying baton during cheerleading practice?' the nurse asks, taking notes.

'No, she fainted due to the overwhelming odour of freshly applied hairspray,' Dylan informs her. 'It was her first time, we should have warned her.'

'Well, she's missed most of the class now,' the nurse says.

'Does that mean it's home time? It's been quite a day . . .' I chip in.

'No, you're well enough to go to the game,' the nurse smiles. 'You have to do your duty as a student of Happyville High!' she says encouragingly. 'Just remember to smile, and if for some reason the grins don't come back, seek medical advice straight away!'

'What, no home time?' I say, looking at the others.

'It's compulsory,' Ashley scowls. 'Compulsory sport . . . I'll let that phrase sink in.'

'Great,' I groan. 'Still, at least we're not *playing* sport, are we? Please tell me we're not playing it!'

'No, just watching,' Dylan says, her head sinking into her shoulders.

'Oh phew, well watching's OK, I mean how bad can it be?'

The force of the crowd hits me full in the face. It's all noise and shouting and people everywhere, and it's ten times worse with a headache. People with scarves and sparkly wigs, people with flags, people in hats—it's like being shot in the eyes by a rainbow made of screams. Everyone is very excited about something. This can't *all* be for sport, surely?

There's a band playing and marching around, although they are doing neither particularly well or in time. It's as if I missed some great life lesson where they explained why sport is so important. As far as I can see, one team wins and one team loses, and occasionally they draw—those are the only outcomes. It's the equivalent of dressing up and having a sing-song for a random game of rock, paper, scissors. Ashley and Dylan tell me the game is American football. Never heard of it.

I put my hands over my ears as we make our way through the crowds to some seats in the stand.

There are cheerleaders throwing pompoms and sticks into the air, and there is twirling, oh Lordy, so much twirling. Suddenly a baton spins overhead like a low-flying helicopter. I just manage to duck out of the way—this is a total safety nightmare! It's all right for those people on the pitch; they have helmets and padding on. I duck again as a pom-pom flies past my ear. Everywhere I look I see spectators on their phones, grinning, laughing, and taking selfies.

Suddenly, for no obvious reason, an air horn goes off and everyone takes their seats.

'You're right, this is awful!' I say to Dylan and Ashley. 'Why are they so excited?'

'We're playing our rivals, springtown wildcats, and for reasons we're not sure about it's very important that we win,' Ashley replies.

'Whatever you do, don't take out a book and read while the game's on. They boo and hiss,' Dylan says, pointing at the crowd.

'How long does it go on for?'

'Hours and hours, but it feels longer,' Dylan sighs.

'At various points the whole thing stops and a load of new players come on to the pitch, at which point people either cheer or boo. Then halfway through, everything stops so the band can play, then if we're lucky our team wins and we can all go home,' Ashley says.

'I wore a helmet to the game one year,' Dylan says, 'but it only seemed to encourage people to throw *more* things at my head.'

'You get a lot of things thrown at your head, don't you Dylan,' I say.

'More than I'd like, yes. Anyway, since then we've been hiding inside the trash cans by the side of the pitch. They're surprisingly roomy . . . are you sure you don't want to reconsider?'

'NO! NO MORE TRASH CANS!' I yell back. 'This may be a complete waste of everyone's time, but we are *not* going to hide. We are going to endure sport if it's the last thing we do,' I announce proudly.

'Wait, did you say endure or enjoy?' Ashley asks.

'The former I think,' Dylan tells her.

'But how?' Ashley asks.

'We are going to blend in. Think of it as an experiment. We are here to observe,' I say wisely.

Dylan grabs her phone from her bag, and begins to type away. 'I've googled some phrases that we can use to make it seem as though we know what we're talking about,' Dylan says, showing us the phone.

'"What a goal", "That ball was never out", "Game, set, and match", and "checkmate",'

I read out. 'I think these are from different games.'

'Well, it can't hurt to try them out,' Dylan shrugs.

Two and a bit cold, long hours later we were still there, standing, cheering, booing, and occasionally yelling out 'checkmate' where it seemed appropriate. Actually playing couldn't be as exhausting as this.

From what I could gather, things were at a very crucial point; our team, and I say 'our team' like I give a flaming hoot, are drawing with the Wildcats and Happyville High have one more chance to throw the ball and win the game.

'**HOTDOGS, GET YOUR HOTDOGS HERE!**'
a boy shouts.

'**EXCUSE ME, DO YOU HAVE ANYTHING VEGAN?**' I call over to him, feeling peckish. Ashley gives me a nudge, '**AND SOMETHING GLUTEN-FREE FOR MY FRIEND HERE?**'

Just then, the cheerleaders start up their chanting and the snack boy turns his attention to the pitch, ignoring my question.

'**GIVE ME A B...**' Courtney yells.

'What does she want a bee for?' I ask. 'She knows you can't just summon bees, right? I mean, you can train any insect in the order Hymenoptera to sniff out explosives, but you can't simply call one to heel like a dog,' I point out.

'She's going to spell out "Blane", the name of the quarterback guy, the one who throws the ball,' Ashley says.

'Oh,' I say, because that makes much more sense. 'The throwing guy, I totally know which one that is!' This is the most sporty I've ever felt in my life, and suddenly I feel quite excited about this whole sport business.

The cheerleaders complete their chant and cartwheel past the players as they make their way back out onto the field. Blane runs out to the centre of the pitch, rubbing his arm. There's talk amongst the spectators that he may be injured; he's been rubbing it throughout the game but so far it seems to be holding up. After some shouting of numbers

that presumably mean something, Blane gets
the ball and looks for someone to throw it
to. The crowd rise to their feet. Blane looks
one way then the other and for a moment
everything seems to stand still. He is about to
be knocked down by the opposition players
when he staggers sideways as though he's
feeling dizzy. We see him shaking his head
and hitting the top of his helmet as though
he was a fly in his ear, before letting out an
almighty yell of '**BOO-YAH!**' He waves his
arm around like a lasso, before jerking it back,
ready to throw the ball in the air.

And that's when something extraordinary
happens. Blane's arm grows. I mean it gets
longer, as though it's made of clay and it's

being stretched. It must be twelve feet long, reaching the height of two men! Suddenly his

arm is flying high above all the other players and there's nothing anyone can do to stop Blane making the

pass. The ball spins through the air, before landing perfectly in the hands of a teammate. There is an utterly stunned silence.

'WE WON! WE WON!'

someone behind me yells as the crowd burst

into applause.

'YES, BUT DID YOU SEE HIS ARM?'

I shriek.

'I KNOW, WHAT A THROW!'

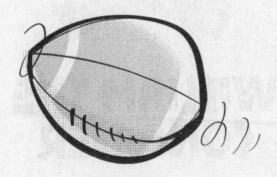

I look over to see Ashley darting under
her seat. '**TOO MUCH COMMUNAL HUGGING.
BRAIN CANNOT COMPUTE!**' she wails.

I look over at Dylan, who grabs my arms
and yells loudly, 'Remember when we said
weird stuff seems to happen a lot and no one
cares? Welcome to Happyville.'

CHAPTER FIVE

WILLIAM THE CONGA-ER

A huge air horn sounds signalling the end of
the game.

'Wait, it can't be over . . . and yes,' I add,
'I am aware that means I want a sporting event
to carry on and that in itself is very strange,
but seriously, what just happened? People's
arms just don't grow ten feet by themselves.
I mean look at it, it looks like it's made of
spaghetti!'

'We told you strange things happen here in Happyville,' Dylan says, looking pleased with herself.

'Yes, but I thought you meant the way people spoke, or that maybe sometimes the TV reception goes a bit odd, not that people's arms grew in front of our very eyes!'

'Well, to be fair, this doesn't happen often, never in fact,' Ashley says.

I feel a bit sick. I appear to have left the city and moved right into the middle of a horror movie. I wonder if it would be too late to move back home? Maybe I could take Ashley and Dylan with me—I could adopt them, like the time I adopted a llama at the zoo. I could send their parents regular updates and photos of their progress. I look around, everyone's still cheering. There's a kid near me who is recording the whole thing on his phone and I decide to be brave and talk to him. 'What's your name?'

'Will,' he yells back, clearly annoyed I have interrupted his chest thumping with his friends.

'Did *you* see what just happened?'

'Err, like totally, it was sweet! Blane dropped the pigskin in the deep man and turned the tide.'

'I'm sorry, I don't mean to be rude, but does that mean "yes"?'

'Yes, it means yes,' he says, looking at me crossly.

'So you saw what happened to Blane's arm?'

'Yeah, it was totally sick!'

'Oh my goodness, you're right! But how did he get sick? What kind of pathogen could cause his arm to grow . . .? Unless it was a mutation?'

Will looks at me blankly. 'Yeah, like totally, what a pass—wham bam thank you Blane the man!'

'Right, oh, I don't know what that means either, never mind.' I turn to Ashley and Dylan. 'I think this town is full of mutants and we have to leave. **RIGHT NOW!**'

'Wait,' Ashley says, 'Blane's about to speak to the crowd.'

Mr Jones is standing on the pitch, holding a microphone up to Blane's face. 'What a game

Blane, talk me through it bro.'

'Well yeah, I mean I was just running out of space when the good old arm came through for me. Go arm!' he shouts as the crowd cheer wildly in the stands. 'I've been working out in the gym and working on my throwing techniques, and I guess it's really paid off. **I MEAN LOOK AT THIS BAD BOY!**' he yells, flexing his muscles.

'What is he talking about?' I whisper to Dylan. 'Your arms don't stretch just by working out a bit.'

'**YOU'RE THE BEST, BLANE, NOW LET'S GET OUR PARTY ON BRO!**' Mr Jones does a chest bump with Blane, and the rest of the team crowd around their star thrower, lifting him on to their shoulders.

'LET'S HAVE A SCHOOL SELFIE, DUDES!'
Mr Jones says, pulling out his camera. Everyone
on the pitch tries to squeeze in. They're all
pouting their lips like they're guppy fish.

'I NEED TO GET OUT OF HERE. I FEEL

SICK!' I cry. 'I never thought I'd say this but
Dad was right—I do need some fresh air!'

'If we walk out now, people will see us.

Celebrating Happyville High's happy victory is compulsory, remember,' Dylan says.

'You're right. We need to get out of here but we need to be smart. Luckily I am. This may be the hardest thing I've ever done. Harder than the time I turned the washing machine into a candyfloss machine with only a screwdriver, a bag of sugar, and a pink felt-tip pen. We just need to blend in,' I say thoughtfully. 'Look, there are wigs and big fake hands discarded all around us. I say we put these on and do a conga.'

'A what?' Ashley asks.

'It's like a human train. I read about it in a book. We do a conga and some cheering, cause a distraction, and sneak out of here.

Shall we?' I say.

Quietly and carefully we set the plan in motion. We place sparkly wigs on top of our heads, we stick big foam hands on our arms, and when we're sure we are completely unrecognizable, we get ready to go for it . . .

'**WAIT!**' Dylan yells, 'I've seen these before, we need a chant, people sing something relevant followed by "**NAH-NAH-NAH-NAH, NAH-NAH, NAH, NAH**".'

Dylan is right again. 'What about the thing that kid in the stands just said?' I say, pointing at Will. 'It was something like, "**WHAM BAM, THANK YOU BLANE THE MAN**". That sounds like it might work.'

'**LET'S DO IT!**' Ashley and Dylan say

together. And so with no conga experience, we set out on our first conga escape.

'**WHAM BAM BLANE IS DA MAN, NAH-NAH-NAH-NAH-NAH-NAH-NAH!**' I shout, rather pleased with my improvisation skills. And it works! Everyone assumes we're joining in the celebrations and no one takes any notice. For a glorious moment it seems we are going to escape! Until I see Will pointing as us, and then I know we are about to be exposed for the nerdy fraudsters that we are.

'**HEY, COOL, A CONGA!**' And just like that he joins on the end. 'Go away!' I hiss from my place at the front. 'This is my conga.'

'No way, the more the merrier!' he cries, beckoning his friends over.

'**JUST KEEP GOING,**' Dylan urges me,
'**DRIVE THIS CONGA HOME!**'

'**ERM GUYS, GUYS!**' Ashley calls out.
'**PERSONAL SPACE ISSUES!**'

'**I CAN'T HEAR YOU, IT'S TOO NOISY, ASHLEY!**' I shout.

We're heading down my road and I can see my house up ahead.

'Erm guys . . .' Ashley says again.

This conga is really heavy—who knew driving it would be so tiring? And the endless chanting has given me a headache. Still we're almost there.

'I really think you should see this,' Ashley calls out.

I turn around and see what Ashley is pointing

at. Drat! So much for sneaking—it seems that the whole school has joined our conga. The line snakes all the way back down the road, probably all the way back to school. I've managed to draw attention to myself by trying not to draw attention to myself.

Maybe, if I can get rid of them all before my

dad sees, it will all be OK? Oh no! Dad's coming out of the garden, looking right at me with a look of bewilderment on his face. I slam on the conga brakes and take off my wig.

'Well, you did tell me to make friends,' I grin nervously.

CHAPTER SIX

ARMY LIKE A SALAMI

'**EVERYONE!**' I yell, '**THIS HAS BEEN FUN, BUT I REALLY THINK YOU NEED TO GO HOME NOW. ERM . . . GO HAPPYVILLE!**' I shout out, pumping my fist.

'**GO HAPPYVILLE NAH-NAH-NAH-NAH, NAH-NAH-NAH-NAH!**' someone at the back of the conga shouts. Everyone does an about-face and the conga starts up all over again, heading back towards school. I grab Dylan and

Ashley and hold them back.

'Come round to mine before school tomorrow. Let's do some research tonight to try and figure out what's really going on here and share our findings over breakfast. What made Blane's arm grow longer? Is this thing a disease? Is it a mutation? Is it contagious? **OH MY GOODNESS, IT COULD BE CONTAGIOUS!**'

'I'll monitor social media—see what the word on the street is,' Dylan says enthusiastically.

'I'll see what I can get from the footage of the game,' adds Ashley.

'Great, I'll do some background stuff on Blane, see if there's anything we're missing. If we can figure out what happened, we might be able to stop it from happening to others. Life is hard enough without having a huge arm to contend with.' We all nod at each other. 'My place, tomorrow morning,' I remind them.

With that we disband, and I turn to my dad who looks as though he can't believe what he's just seen.

'Is that normal? I mean, to conga home on your first day?' he asks.

'Dad, I can confidently say that there is nothing normal about this school, or indeed this whole town. The most normal things about this place are Ashley, Dylan, and myself,' I sigh.

'Oh right.' Dad smiles a worried smile. 'Erm, anyway—I have some exciting news! My tomato plants are thriving. I swear they're growing in front of my very eyes!' He pulls out his phone and shows me all the selfies he's been taking with his plants, as if they're his children.

'Hey, maybe we should put some compost in your shoes, make you grow a couple of feet overnight, too!'

I stare at Dad, an idea forming. 'Not today, thanks. I think I'm just going to go to my room. I have a lot of fashion homework to catch up on.'

'Oh OK, great! I'll bring a sandwich up for you later, after I've mowed the lawn. It's not quite the right height to create maximum happiness,' he smiles.

I grab a book off my shelf, *The Manure, Compost, and Fertilizer Encyclopedia* and lie on my bed—there must be a way of stopping this long-arm business before it gets out of hand. But I feel so tired after everything that's happened today . . . the conga line, and all that chanting at the American football match . . .

I wake up with a start. There's a book over my face and I can hear banging on the door of my bedroom.

'**FITZ! FITZ!!!**' It's Dylan and Ashley.

'**YEAH, COME IN!**' I yell back. There's a creak as the door of my bedroom swings open. I peel the book off my face.

'**MORNING!**' Ashley says. 'Whoa, nice furniture. I like the minimal look—it says "functional, but not indulgent". Tell me, were you inspired by the Bauhaus movement?'

'No, silly, she just hasn't unpacked the cardboard boxes yet,' Dylan chuckles.

'Coffee . . . I need coffee,' I say in the manner of a person who's been crawling across the desert looking for a cup of water.

'Coffee later,' Dylan cries out. 'You need to pick up when I call!'

'Sorry, I must have fallen asleep, I was

working on a wild theory that—'

'That Blane might have eaten compost thinking it was some sort of nutritious protein powder?' Dylan interrupts.

'Yeah, how did you know?' I ask, dumbstruck.

'The text from the book you were reading must have rubbed off on to your cheek when you were asleep. I don't think that theory is correct though,' Dylan says, shaking her head.

'Impressive,' I say, 'and also, I agree: the theory doesn't add up. I mean who would eat compost thinking it was food?'

'Exactly. Anyway, forget Blane, he's old news,' Dylan says and then stops short. 'Hang on, I'm looking around but I can't see a computer anywhere.

WHERE'S THE COMPUTER? WHERE?!

Her voice is suddenly filled with panic.

'Dylan, we've talked about this,' Ashley

says, trying to calm her down. 'Go to your

happy place.' Ashley takes Dylan's hands and

makes her close her eyes. 'Repeat after me,

"my name's Dylan and I don't always need to

be near a computer".' Dylan repeats the mantra

over and over. Ashley looks over at me and

whispers, 'We need to get her to a computer,

she's in withdrawal.'

'OK,' I nod, putting on my dressing gown.

'Let's go to the den.'

'Hey there, Peachy Pie!' Dad smiles as we

walk through the kitchen. He's already in his

gardening gear and it looks as though he's

been up for hours. 'I let your friends in, I hope

you don't mind?'

'No worries, Dad. Could I get a double

macchiato to go?' I ask.

'No, you can have cereal and juice like

everyone else your age.' He smiles back.

One day, one day he'll make me one.

I grab a bowl of cereal and a cup of juice

and open the back door, showing Ashley and

Dylan the trailer in the garden, glinting like a

spaceship in the sun. 'That's my den,' I smile.

'Does it—?' Dylan begins to ask.

'Yes it does, and not just one computer, but several . . .' But Dylan's already off like a greyhound out of the traps, her little legs hurtling towards the end of the garden.

'How often does she get like this?' I ask Ashley as we stroll down after her.

'She's better than she used to be. I think she has dependence issues: she wasn't cuddled as a baby, or she was cuddled too much, I forget. Every so often I have to calm her down. I can't believe I had to touch her hands.'

We arrive at the den and Dylan is already there, hugging a computer. I shoot Ashley a look.

'Like I said, she's better than she used to be.' Ashley raises an eyebrow at me.

Dylan fires up the computer and starts typing away, like a great pianist at a grand piano, she's completely and utterly at home.

'So what did I miss?' I say, still trying to wake up.

'It all happened late last night,' Ashley says. 'I was watching a video of the game on YouTube, trying to break down the footage frame by frame when someone posted a comment: "amazing arm, man, same thing happened to me after the game." So I tracked the comment down to another kid at school called Carlton. Here's what he posted.'

Dylan clicks on a photo. I see a smiling schoolboy, posing with his head in his hand, looking normal except for the fact that his other arm is draped on the floor like a big fleshy draught excluder.

'**ARGH!**' I yell. 'What does the post say?'

Dylan squints and begins to read: 'Look at my massive arm, hashtag yeah, hashtag

big arm, hashtag army-like-a-salami, hashtag
. . . do you want me to read all the hashtags
because I think there are about thirty of them?'

'This makes no sense at all,' I say.

'I know, I'm not sure when hashtags
became a way of communicating. It's a sign
that civilization is declining,' Ashley pipes up.

'No, not that, I mean we've definitely
discounted the compost theory: there's no way
that *two* people could eat compost by mistake.
Two people can't be that stupid.'

'Neither can three,' Ashley says, shaking
her head and showing me her phone. 'This is
Kendall, she posted about three hours ago,
again, same sort of thing about a massive arm,
then a deluge of hashtags and selfies. So I set

my phone up to get alerts any time someone uses the hashtag "army-like-a-salami", and that's when things started to go crazy.'

'Oh my, how many in total?'

'Thirteen,' Dylan says, turning to look at me.

'THIRTEEN! ALL LIKE BLANE?!'

Dylan nods, 'All in Happyville, all within the past twenty-four hours.'

'Has anyone called an ambulance or a doctor?' I shriek.

'Why would they?' Ashley asks.

'They love it,' Dylan says.

'What? How?'

'I think you need to come with us,' Ashley says, putting her arm round me. 'Grab your scooter and let us show you exactly what sort of place we're living in.'

'I'll just get dressed!' I say, rushing back to my room. These two have no idea that I've never really used my scooter before, but hey, this is in an emergency.

'Wait a minute, off so soon?' Dad asks as I grab my scooter from the hallway. Oh no! Just as I suspected, Dad is going to try and 'make conversation'. He wants to talk to my friends, doesn't he? He's going to do it—he's going to pretend to be cool.

'So I was watching MTV the other day,' he says with a swagger. Oh no, it's too late, he's already started.

'Erm, we're kind of in a hurry, algebra

breakfast club!' I say, trying to get away.

'Tell me Ashley, Dylan, do you like the old MTV?' he continues. Ashley and Dylan nod uncertainly, shooting panicked glances at one another.

'Televisions are basically mini particle accelerators, or the old-fashioned ones were at least. Do you have a new TV or an old one?' Ashley asks boldly.

'New. There was a great band on there the other day, they reminded me of the Rolling Stones in many ways, they had guitars and they were singing, it sort of went like this . . .'

PLEASE DON'T SING, PLEASE DON'T SING, PLEASE DON'T SING! I scream to myself.

'**LALLALALLALALALALALALALALA!**' Dad

screeches. Not only that but he also plays a bit

of air guitar. Oh the agony!

'Do you know it?' Dad asks.

'I only like jazz,' Ashley says, 'it's like

listening to pure maths, I find the frivolous

nature of pop culture stomach-turning.'

There's an awkward pause and then Dad says, 'Well, I'd best go, maybe you girls would like to come round for supper sometime? I've been growing some excellent beets and squashes! Happyville has a vegetable club—I think I might join. You know what they say— happy vegetables are tasty vegetables!'

'Maybe. I'm allergic to most things— perhaps I'll send you a list. I'm pretty good with boiled rice though. Do you have boiled rice? All you need really is rice and a kettle,' Ashley says, trying to be helpful.

'Well, I'll see what I can do,' Dad says, looking a bit deflated.

'I like pop tarts!' Dylan grins.

'Pop tarts and rice, rightio,' Dad says,

making a mental note.

'Can we go now?' I say, after leaving the silence hanging in the air just longer than is comfortable.

'Of course, Peach,' he smiles. 'Have a great day at school, kids.' He hands me my packed lunch and we head on out.

'Right, where to?' I ask, not sure what I'm expecting to see.

'Follow us,' Ashley says, jumping on her scooter. 'Wow, your dad is really intense.' Ashley looks over her shoulder at my maniacally waving Dad.

'He can be—he's mostly all right. I'm training him up and one day he may reach the dizzy heights of not being annoying.'

'Well, I thought he was cool,' says Dylan, catching up. 'Who was he?'

'He was my dad, who did you think he was?'

'Oh I dunno, maybe like a musician or the chef,' she says.

'A musician? What do you mean chef? I don't have a chef!'

'Well, he seemed to know an awful lot about food. And then he gave you your lunch—coincidence?' Dylan says, letting the question hang in the air.

'Yes!' I look at Ashley who rolls her eyes. Was it me or did she also look a bit relieved that she wasn't the only one who had to deal with Dylan these days.

'I have two older brothers,' Dylan went on obliviously. 'They like guitar music. Sometimes they even let me listen to it. I mean, from the other side of the door, but if I listen closely with a glass I can hear what they're listening to. I'm not allowed in their room or allowed to talk to them really, they say I'm too much of a nerd. Both of them work with my mum and dad in the bakery in town. It means I get free cakes, which is great, but they work really long hours so it also means I spend a lot of time on my own. But that's OK, I have computers! You don't need parents when you have computers. If I feel like I don't know what to do, I just YouTube a video on parenting. That way it's like I have a mum and dad, but they live in a computer . . . maybe that's why I like computers so much?' Dylan smiles cheerfully.

'That could be it,' I say. 'OK then . . . what about you, Ashley?' I ask.

'I have seven cats,' she says. 'I have tracking devices on all of them to see where they go, and what they do.'

'Oh, what do they do?' I ask.

'Mostly sleep, so I've introduced a caffeine-enriched diet to liven them up,' she says, getting her phone out to show me.

'Mum and dad?' I ask, and she pauses for a second as if trying to remember.

'Affirmative,' she nods. 'I've fitted a tracking device to them too if you're interested?'

'Erm, maybe later.'

'How about you?' Dylan asks.

'Just me and Dad. It's been that way for a long time,' I answer.

Suddenly Ashley stamps on her scooter brake and all three of us come to a halt.

'There, this is what I wanted to show you.'

It's still early, school doesn't start for another half hour, but the town is coming to life. We're in the middle of the town square, the heart of Happyville. It's like everything else in this town: perfect like a painting, but one done by numbers. It's immaculate but somehow cold and soulless. There are shops around the square—all the sort you'd expect—an old-fashioned diner, and a bakery, which I realize must be Dylan's parents' place.

Further up, there's a kid helping an old lady get her cat out of a tree. I look over to the other side of the street, where a girl wearing an apron is watering the hanging baskets outside the coffee shop. Inside the grocery store, another girl is reaching for something on the top shelf.

Except the boy rescuing the cat is just standing there while his six-foot arm pulls the cat down; the girl watering the baskets isn't using a chair or a ladder, just a giant limb holding the watering can; and the other girl is taking a candy bar from the top shelf of the next aisle along, as her arm squiggles over the top of other shoppers going about their business.

And are people screaming? Are people running away at the sight of these long-armed youths about town? Oh no, they are just smiling as though this is perfectly OK, it's just the latest fashion, as harmless as a new haircut.

'What's wrong with these people?' I hiss to Dylan and Ashley. 'I could turn up to school wearing last season's shoes or something and everyone would recoil and point at me like I was a witch in the Middle Ages. And yet people walk around with freakishly long arms and no one says anything?' I can't believe what I'm seeing!'

'I reckon they think of it as an

upgrade. You upgrade your phone so why not your arm?' Ashley says, shaking her head.

'Arm 2.0,' Dylan shrugs.

'Well, I don't want to end up with an arm like a giraffe's neck. Imagine trying to buy sweaters! We need to figure out what's going on. This all started with Blane, right?' I say. 'We need to track him down and ask him a few questions. He's the source of this outbreak or whatever this is, so he must hold the answer.'

'Blane's never going to talk to *us*. He's one

of *them*. People like that don't talk to people like us,' Dylan whispers.

'If you like I could play progressive jazz at him until he cracks?' Ashley suggests. 'It worked on my dad when he tried to hide my birthday present as a surprise. That'll teach him to try and inject fun into what is effectively a countdown until death.'

'No, we need something else. We need to be on the inside. We need to be like them,' I say.

'Oh great, you're going to make us dress up again, aren't you?' Ashley sighs.

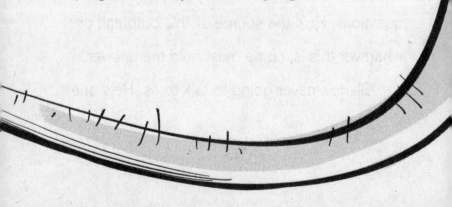

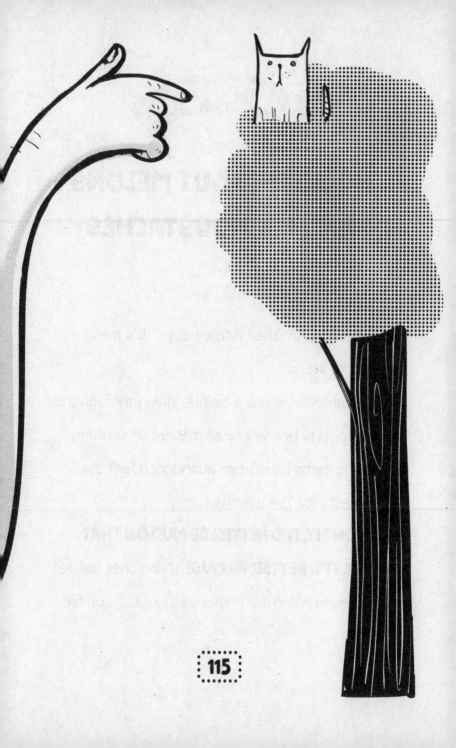

HOLLOWED OUT MELONS AND BIG MOUSTACHES

'This plan is insane,' Ashley says. 'It's never going to work.'

Granted, she has a point—sifting through the lost-property box where all manner of sporting clothing items have been abandoned isn't the brightest idea I've ever had.

'OH MY, IT'D BETTER BE MUD ON THAT SHIRT, IT'D BETTER BE MUD!' Dylan cries before Frisbee-ing it into the corner as though it's on fire.

'Listen, this isn't my idea of fun either, in fact the thought of putting other people's clothes on makes me wince. But I'll remind you again, if any of us actually owned any appropriate sportswear this wouldn't be a problem. But we don't own a shin pad between us, so while rummaging through lost property isn't ideal, we need to do it—it's the only way to get close to Blane. Now Ashley, are you sure we're not going to get into trouble for missing lessons?'

'Leave it with me, the receptionist is easy to manipulate. I can handle her,' Ashley assures us.

'Great, slightly creepy, but great,' I reply.

A few more minutes of rummaging and we

finally have everything we need. 'This may well work in our favour,' I say. 'With these helmets and pads, no one will know it's us. We just need to sound like people who play sport. Call each other bro, slap each other on the back, be gruff, and holler a lot. Basically just do impressions of farmyard animals and we'll be fine. Let's get our kit on, it's time for phase two.'

A few moments later we are all kitted up and heading for reception.

We stroll up to the receptionist's desk and hit the bell. 'Leave the talking to me,' Ashley says confidently.

'Yes.' A woman suddenly appears from

round the corner. She's caked in make-up and
has a smile like a constipated shark.

'Trisha. May I call you Trisha?' Ashley says,
looking at the woman's name tag. 'I guess
if you didn't want me to call you Trisha, you
wouldn't have written it on your name tag.

Here's the thing, me and my two friends here are going to take a day off from lessons, to try out for the football team. We're going to play sports in order to get closer to Blane and work out the mystery of his long arm, which is also why we're wearing these ridiculous disguises. Is that okay, Trisha?'

Dylan and I look at each other nervously.

'So I want you to go and tell your bosses, the faceless pen-pushing bureaucrats who run this corporation they call a school, that we won't be in our lessons today. We are unplugging from the matrix and going rogue. Got that, Trisha?'

Trisha looks at us blankly.

'We're not going to lessons today, we're

playing sport,' Ashley tells her in plain and simple terms.

Understanding dawns on Trisha's face and she hands us our free passes.

'Thank you, Trisha,' Ashley says, grabbing the passes and handing them out. 'You have shown great ingenuity, demonstrating that you are more than just another foot soldier in their tyrannical war. Come the revolution, we will look favourably on you.'

'Wow!' I can't help but say.

'Thank you, Trisha!' Dylan grins, before adding, 'I like your nails, they sparkle in the sunlight!'

'Do you think it was a wise move to tell her the plan?' I whisper as Ashley marches us off.

'The truth is like jazz, sometimes it's the only way.'

'OK . . . I think. Let's go to the library, there's something else we need to do before playing sports,' I say.

We open the door to the library, slowly and carefully. I don't know why though, since there's never anyone in there apart from us.

'Why are we here? Blane's not going to be in the library, I don't think he can even spell "book", let alone read one,' Ashley says.

'I thought it might be useful to learn the rules of American football before we try and play American football.'

'Hmm, good point,' Dylan nods enthusiastically.

'Having watched the game yesterday, I think we all know the basics. Each team takes it in turns to get the ball into the end zone bit,' I say, grabbing a piece of chalk and drawing on the board. 'They can run with the ball, or throw it. Each team has a thrower . . .'

'**QUARTERBACK!**' Dylan yells. 'I know that, I know that! Wait, are we actually going to play? I thought maybe some strategic standing at the side of the pitch might be good enough.' Dylan's face fills with panic. 'Can't we just ask Blane why his arm grew?'

'This is Blane we're talking about! We'll never get close unless he thinks we're one of them,' I say.

'If one of us can get close enough, we can

123

get a DNA sample,' Ashley says. 'That way we might be able to figure out the mutation which caused the long arm and therefore the answer to this puzzle.'

'Did you *see* the game? They were hurting each other, on purpose! At one point someone left the field because his head fell off!' Dylan cries out.

'No one's head fell off. He had a twisted knee, that's not the same thing,' I say.

'Twisted knee, head, it's all the same. It's all a world of pain. I have an allergy to physical exercise, remember! I come out in hives and throw up.' Dylan's actually shaking now.

'Life is but a blink in the universe's eye. If I have to lay down my life in the name of science, so be it. Having said that, my glasses are steaming up just thinking about it,' Ashley admits a little nervously.

'No one is going to die, I can promise you that. But it might help if we learn about the game, so we won't get hurt!' I say brightly. 'Or at least not *as* hurt.'

'Can we really learn how to play American football in half an hour?' Ashley asks.

'It'll be fine! We're super-clever—how hard can it be?' I say confidently.

'All right, I'm in,' mumbles Dylan. 'We've got enough equipment hidden in the wall to make a basic DNA profiling kit. I mean, it's not sophisticated enough to clone anyone, but it'll do the job.'

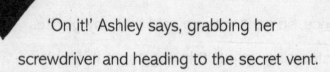

'On it!' Ashley says, grabbing her
screwdriver and heading to the secret vent.

'Dylan and I will have a look round here for
an American football rule book. Practice starts in
thirty minutes! The more we know the safer we'll
be, so let's start looking.'

'Well I never knew there were so many books
written about sport!' I say loudly. 'People must
really like it.' I leaf through each book trying to
find anything I can find on football.

'I know! I've never been to this part of
the library before,' Dylan says, looking around
as though she's found a whole new world to
explore. 'Oh lovely, chess . . .' Dylan pulls out a
book from the shelf.

'We don't have time for fun, Dylan, we need to press on.'

'Sorry, it's just that I've designed a game based on chess in my head, but it's in four dimensions. I'm just trying to figure out how to build the board . . . maybe we could have a game sometime?' she asks.

'Sure, wait, here it is!' I yell, waving a copy of *A Gentleman's Guide to American Football* triumphantly in the air. 'How are you getting on Ashley?' I call over to the secret vent.

'All done!' Ashley announces, waving what looks like a metal shoebox with buttons, lights, and wires all over it. Not only is it functional but it also looks cool.

We open the book and pore over the details.

'It's a bit old-fashioned,' Ashley says. 'It's from 1823!' she exclaims, looking at the print date.

'Sure, but I mean apart from the players having big moustaches and the helmets being made out of what looks like hollowed-out melons, the game hasn't changed that much from what I can tell,' I say, feeling a little unsure.

'There's a section on what to do if someone's spine pops out!' Dylan cries.

'Moving on . . .' I say quickly. 'There are sections on huddles, conversions, touchdowns, and penalties too. It's pretty basic: the team has to get the ball from one side to this end zone thingy, and if they do, they get to kick it between the sticks and win some points. Right?' I say to Dylan.

'Yes, but how do we get the ball down there? Say we start here, like in this diagram, next to the gentleman lying on the ground with a spear in his back . . . how old did you say this book was? Anyway, the question is, how do we get it down the other end?' Dylan says.

'Just launch the ball at 34.8 miles per hour

at an angle of forty-five degrees and it will land here,' Ashley says, peering at the book over Dylan's shoulder.

'What?' I say.

'Just launch—' she begins again.

'Of course!' I cry out. And then, in a moment of pure joy, I do it, I say it: '**EUREKA! ASHLEY, YOU'RE A GENIUS!**'

'I know that. We all know that,' she shrugs.

I grab the book and hold it in front of Dylan. 'This isn't a playbook, it's a math problem. That's how we solve it! It's chess in three dimensions!' I cry out.

'Of course!' Dylan grins. 'It's just a question of assessing the game, working out the probabilities in our heads, running a few possible outcomes, and finding the best option to maximize the most positive result!' she laughs.

'Girls, we can do this! Let's get out there and get Blane's DNA using theorems, algebra, and logarithms.' I attempt a group high five . . .

'OUCH!'

'ARGH MY EYE!'

'EEEK!'

'OK, NO MORE HIGH FIVES.'

CHAPTER EIGHT

BURGERS IN A PICKLE

'I see we've got three new burgers to try out
for the team!' the coach yells at us.

I can tell he's the coach because his hat,
trousers, and sweater all say '**COACH**' on them.
Dylan, Ashley, and I head for the field moving
our legs and arms around in the manner
of people who are trying to do warm up
things. Ashley hangs back and pops the **DNA
PROFILING BOX** by the ice box.

'I've just got to stretch off a bit first!'
Ashley barks out in a silly deep voice, before
yelling '**HELL YEAH!**' between lunges. 'I
cracked a few bones last week and I've still
got some blood in my fingernails!' Ashley looks
over to me. 'Too much?' she whispers.

'A little,' I reply.

'Well you're a feisty little burger, aren't
you?' the coach cries, pointing at Ashley. 'Do
you hear that boys? These guys wanna play
tough.'

The rest of the team circle round us like
we're lobsters in a fish tank and they're about
to order lunch.

'Why does he keep calling us "burgers"?'
I say to the nearest guy, who is huge by the

way. I mean he looks like a rhino, but less sophisticated. Please let him be on my team, please!

'He calls you "burgers", because that's what you are: meat for him to mould.' The guy pops his mouthguard in and wipes the beads of sweat off his enormous pumpkin-head.

'That's it, I'm off. I don't feel so good,' Dylan says, turning to go back the way she just came.

'Not so fast, Dylan.' I grab her by the collar and pull her along as I head towards the rest of the players, who are all really big and look very heavy. They all looked so silly and tiny from far away, but now I'm standing next to them, with their pads and hats—I mean helmets—they look like Easter Island statues, come to life. I need to say something to make me seem not petrified. Like I belong. Think, Fitz, think!

'I can't wait to do a catch goal in the score zone and kick the pigskin between the point sticks! Can I get a whoop-whoop?' I try to shout but it comes out as a strangled shriek.

'NOW THAT'S WHAT I'M TALKING ABOUT! I SEE THIS BURGER IS FLAME-GRILLED!' the coach bellows back. I've no idea what that means. The entire team looks at me.

'You can learn something from this new recruit,' he barks.

On the positive side, the coach now likes me, but on the negative, everyone in the team now hates me. Ah, life's rich tapestry, you really can't beat it. I feel Dylan glaring at me and I turn to face her.

'OK, so I might have gone a bit over the top,' I say.

'MY HIVES! MY HIVES ARE FLARING UP!' she cries.

'Oh my,' Ashley says, looking closely at Dylan's face. 'We've got a stage three eruption going on, Dylan.'

But we don't have time to do anything before the coach shouts out: 'Time to get this game going. Everyone this side of the line is on Blane's team, the rest, well good luck! Now let's toss a few balls with that special arm of yours, and see what happens.'

'Keep your eyes on Blane,' I say urgently to Dylan and Ashley. 'It appears we're on the other team, but that's good—it means we can get close to him. Remember, we have to get the ball into Blane's end zone, and they have to get it into ours. Anyone who gets close to Blane, grab some of his hair . . .'

'How are we supposed to do that without him noticing?' Dylan asks.

'Well, I don't know, use your imagination!'

'I knew I should have brought scissors,' Dylan huffs.

'Scissors on a sports field?' Ashley cries. 'It's like you *want* to be a maverick, Dylan. You need to think straight!'

'You know, I was happy in the library. No

one bothered me in the library. Now look at me, Fitz. **I'M A BURGER! YOU'VE MADE ME A BURGER!** I told you I have athlemaphobia. I'm allergic to physical activity, it makes me nauseous,' Dylan shouts. 'Last time I played tiddlywinks I vomited like a geyser in Yellowstone Park and my face looked like a pizza.'

'Shush!' I urge her, not wanting her to blow our cover. 'We're doing this for science and we're so close. Remember, Dylan, this isn't sport, this is math, that's all. Math on the move while wearing helmets. I know we can do this.'

Suddenly everyone crouches down in a row. They pass the ball through their legs to Blane and then there's mayhem. Players are running, bumping into each other, falling over, and screaming—and before I know which way to turn the play has stopped.

'Can I open my eyes yet?' Dylan whimpers, as she slowly opens them and looks around.

'What just happened?' Ashley says.

'I don't know. Blane had the ball and everyone on our team got very annoyed about the whole thing,' I say.

'YO BURGERS!'

'I think that's us,' I say, 'Yes Mr Coach, sir?'

'WHAT WAS THAT?' he barks. **'THAT WAS TERRIBLE!'**

'He really shouldn't answer his own questions,' I mutter.

'Yes it was!' I shriek back. 'I'm sorry,

I thought we were playing American football here, but that wasn't football, that was a mess. If Army McArmface had any wits about him he would have passed the ball to this guy!' I point to Rhino-boy next to me. 'I was expecting a game here, not a game of baby . . . ball . . . for babies . . . like a load of babies . . .' Why can't I stop saying 'babies'? I cringe into my helmet.

'I was kinda open,' Rhino-boy agrees.

'**DAGNABBIT!**' the coach yells, which I'm not sure is actually a word, but there we go.

'Let's go out there and break some spleens,' he cries.

'He's so angry! Why is he so angry?' Dylan cries. 'Uh-oh, I'm starting to feel sick.'

'Here you go, Flame-grilled! Show them

how it's done,' the coach shouts, throwing the ball at me.

'What are we going to do?' Dylan asks. She's gone quite green now.

'OK, this is like a straight-forward combustion reaction,' I say breathlessly. 'I'll be the oxygen. Ashley you can be the fuel, and Dylan, you bring the heat.'

'OK,' Dylan smiles. 'It's just a 3D math puzzle. Don't puke, don't puke.'

'**BOOOOOOOM!**' I cry. Everyone looks confused. '**HUT!**' I try instead and the ball comes flying at me from between someone's legs. I close my eyes and hold out my hands, and what do you know, it sticks. I have the ball! Right, I need to think like a molecule.

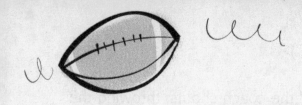

I'm oxygen! I run around in a circle for a bit. It seems to unnerve the other players as they all chase me, bumping into each other. I look downfield and see that Ashley has sprinted off, drawing away some of the opposition and creating the perfect opening for Dylan. Then I see Dylan, wearing an awful lot of heavy American football padding, but running as fast as she possibly can. I calculate her speed using the markings on the field and hurl the ball. It flies through the air at a perfect forty-five degree angle. I see Blane, running backwards with his arm in the air. But

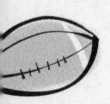

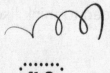

Dylan also holds her hands up and it lands!
A perfect catch and a touchdown! I did a
sports thing! Dylan turns around and grins,
just as Blane comes to a skidding crash at her
feet. We did it. We really did it! Dylan looks
at Blane and in one glorious cheering hiccup
barfs all over him.

'What did you do that for? Is it not
enough you scored? You barfed all over my
beautiful helmet!' he cries, ripping it off in
horror.

'Oops,' Dylan shrugs. 'Let me help you.'
And she swiftly pulls some of his hairs out.

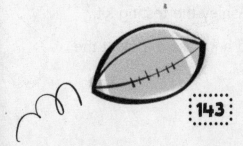

'OW! YOU **BARFED** ON ME AND NOW YOU'RE PULLING MY HAIR OUT!'

'That's more like it!' the coach yells, running over. 'I want us to barf on our opponents and pull their hair out! That's how Happyville High rolls from now on! Session over, boys! **WHOOP!**'

'Well, thanks for the game, gotta fly!' Dylan says, grabbing the **DNA PROFILING KIT** and running over towards Ashley and me.

'Did you get it?' I ask Dylan as we run off the field together. She nods and hands me the hairs, and Ashley the testing kit. I take my helmet off and take a look at the golden strands.

'Finally, I have a lock of Blane's hair!' I grin.

'You have what?' I hear someone growl in my ear.

'Courtney!' I gasp, 'it's not what it looks like!'

'Are you after my man?' she rages.

CHAPTER NINE

BOO-YAH!

'**NO!**' I yell, 'I'm not after your man, I promise!'

Courtney is surrounded by her cheerleading friends: two other girls and a boy. They all have pursed lips and mean looks in their eyes. They look like a vicious gang, but a gang that might attack you with synchronized dancing rather than actual violence.

'It's nice to see you again, Courtney,' I add nervously when she doesn't say anything.

Why does this girl keep following me? It's like we can't stay away from each other. My mind starts whirring. It's like one of those movies where there are two cops who are thrown together and they hate each other at first, but then become best friends. Maybe Courtney will become my best friend? But we have so little in common . . . she might try to do my hair or take me to the mall to go shopping. Wouldn't that be just awful? Maybe we're not like two cops thrown together, maybe we're like a superhero and an arch-nemesis, I'm Brain Girl and she's Courtney the Beautiful and her hairdryer is a ray gun and she's out to destroy me.

'Well then why are you following him

around?' sneers one of Courtney's friends,
jolting me back into the room.

'Good question, Tiffany,' says Courtney.
'What are you following Blane around for, why
are you in disguise, and why, oh why, do you
have a lock of his hair?'

In many ways these are all good questions. It isn't as simple as a math equation though, is it? Where do you learn the answers to problems like these? I look at Dylan and Ashley but they both look totally clueless. If I tell Courtney I'm trying to figure out why her boyfriend is a freak, then she's probably going to hold it against me.

'Hey Courtney, funny story . . .' Dylan starts, playing for time. 'We were on our way to a fancy dress party when—'

'No you weren't,' Courtney snaps. 'I want to hear it from her. And *what* is wrong with your face?'

'I have hives but now I've puked they should calm down,' Dylan replies.

149

'Well?' Courtney asks me, turning away from Dylan in disgust.

I'm going to have to say it. 'Fine, I wanted to get a closer look at Blane's arm . . .'

'Did you hear that, Courtney? She wants a ticket to his gun show! The little creep has a thing for him!' shouts the slick-haired boy standing next to Courtney.

'Gun show? Are you referring to Blane's arms as guns? No, I just want to know why his arm grew so big. You have to admit, it is a bit creepy.'

'Creepy?' Courtney looks horrified. 'What's creepy is that you'd do anything to try and steal my boyfriend. He has a long arm because he's a fashion leader. It's the latest trend, like remember there was a time when people used to wear socks with flip-flops?'

'Yeah, I've seen photographic proof. I nearly puked my eyeballs out,' Tiffany interrupts.

'Yeah, anyway, we don't do that any more, thank goodness, but don't you see? Things change. Sometimes it's big handbags, sometimes smaller ones. Socks with flip-flops, no socks with flip-flops. He's just very fashion conscious. That's why I totally dig him,' she explains.

'Someone's arm growing abnormally long is not the same as a big handbag!' I cry.

'Hey, what's that your dorky friend's carrying?' Tiffany says, looking at Ashley's DNA profiling kit. 'It says "Property of Happyville High" on it. Have you been stealing from the school?' she scowls. 'I'm not sure how the principal would feel about that . . .'

Ashley hides it behind her back and shoots me a look. If we lose the tester, then the whole thing will have been a waste of time. I need to distract Courtney and her gang, and there's only one thing I can think of to do.

'You're right, Courtney, I do have a thing for your boyfriend. Blane's just so interested in his own face and hair . . . it's such a lovely quality. I also like his brain; it's such a mystery what's going on in there. He's really interesting and I like his sporting talents too . . .' Is Courtney buying any of this? ' . . . so anyway, I

persuaded my friends to dress up like athletes
so that I could stalk him and get a lock of
his beautiful hair to add to the Blane shrine I
have in my house, even though I only met him
yesterday. He has no idea, so please don't say
anything to him. I am very sorry, I realize all
this may sound a bit weird, and in fact saying
it out loud it sounds very weird too. I realize it
was a mistake and I need to take a long hard
look at myself. I'm sorry, Courtney. I promise
it won't happen again. It's time to escape this
web of lies. Please can you forgive me?' I close
my eyes and await the inevitable thump on the
nose.

'Well, it better not happen again, Fitz.
I'm going to be watching you all very

CLOSELYAAAAAAAAAAAAAAAARGHGAHGAGH!'

Courtney wails.

'I'm sorry, what?' Dylan asks.

'Nothing, I meant to say "closely" . . . I feel weird, does anyone else feel weird?' Courtney asks.

'Maybe it was the skinny latte you had. Perhaps the soya milk was a little off, honey,' the other girl says. She's the one who isn't Tiffany, so I'll just pretend she's called Tiffany Two.

'No, it's my arm, it feels heavy and tingly,' Courtney says, looking at her hand. We all take a step back. Ashley pulls out her phone and begins to record.

'**O** to the **M** to the **G!**' Tiffany yells excitedly,

clapping her hands. 'I think it might be happening. Does it hurt?'

'No . . . I just, just . . . JUST . . . just feel a little unusual . . . **WOOOOOOOWAAAAAAAAH!** It's like I have pins and needles and my arm's waking up, strange but nice but horrible but **WEEEEEEEEEEIRD!**'

Just at that second Courtney begins to scratch her arm and wave it around like a lasso. Then her face goes pouty and her lips stick out like a fish.

'This is fantastic evidence,' says Ashley. 'Can you look this way, Courtney? The light's better over here . . . that's it, give me angry, give me that big beautiful arm . . . not too close, I don't like being crowded.'

'I think I'm going to puke again,' Dylan says, holding her stomach.

Courtney's eyes roll around in her head and then she cries, '**BOO-YAH!**' She holds her arm straight up in the air and then, like something out of *Jack and the Beanstalk*, it shoots three feet in the air, right in front of our eyes! It is amazing, also awful, and I'm slightly disappointed there is no funny sound like in a *Tom and Jerry* cartoon. Courtney shakes herself like she's waking from a dream. She's staring at her arm as though it doesn't even belong to her.

'Oh man, I am *so* jealous. I was hoping that

I'd be next!' Tiffany Two sighs.

'It totally suits you,' Tiffany says, eyeing her up and down like she's a fashion model.

'I've gone full army-like-a-salami. Wait till I tell Blane, he's going to be super-psyched about this. Just think of all the selfies we can take!' Courtney smiles as though she's just won the lottery. 'This is the single greatest thing that's ever happened to me!'

Courtney looks at me and grabs me by the scruff of my neck, hoisting me in the air. I shriek as she holds me high above the ground, dangling me like a fish on a rod. Hmm, can I see my house from here?

No wait, better concentrate on not dying.

'I'll let the shrine thing go, I mean who hasn't got one of those?' Courtney snarls.

'I have two!' the slick-haired boy interrupts.

'But if I ever see you near my boyfriend again I will snap you like a breadstick— understand?' she says.

I nod, then she drops me. 'Ouch!' I cry.

'Are you OK?' Dylan asks.

'Yes, just about. Ashley, can you stop filming now?'

'It's research. Scientific research.'

After smuggling our disguises back into lost property, getting changed, and putting the DNA profiling kit carefully into Ashley's backpack, we are on our scooters and racing back home.

'We'll meet back at my den at eight o'clock to figure this whole thing out once and for all,' I say.

The sky is getting dark as we head through the town square and say our goodbyes as we each peel off in different directions.

Wherever I look on my journey home I see people with huge long arms or see them transforming before my eyes. Distant yells of '**BOO-YAH!**' fill the air. If we don't do something fast, the whole of the world may well end up like this.

CHAPTER TEN

LAWN AND ORDER

As I crash through the gate, something strikes me as odd. The lawn; it's so neat.

'Hey there, young lady,' a voice floats from over the fence. It's Jean.

'Hello Jean, how are you?' I ask.

'Well, I'm just fine. Hey, hasn't your dad done a great job with the lawn? We are sticklers for neatness. It's a fact that a well-manicured lawn makes everyone happier! Your dad is going to fit in perfectly!' she says with a happy smile. 'Tell me dear, why don't you have one of those long arms that all the kids have these days? I remember when skateboards first arrived in Happyville. Of course they turned out to be far too dangerous and noisy for this sort of town, but it was exciting for a while.'

'I don't have one of those arms yet, because . . . well, I don't know. But I'm going to find out soon. Bye, Jean!' I head inside and see Dad studying a colour chart.

'Hey Peachy, can you tell me what shade of green I should choose for the lawn? I like "Applicious" but I think Jean's is "Keen Green" so maybe we should try and match hers.' Dad inspect a sample of grass through a magnifying glass.

Dad is making me nervous. He's never been this fastidious about grass before. 'Are you OK? I mean, I like that you're into gardening but I'm not sure it matters what colour the grass is. Anywhere in the ballpark of green is fine; the lawn police are fairly tolerant.'

'The lawn police, are they here?' he asks, panicking.

'I was joking, there's no such thing as the lawn police, Dad.' But he picks up a leaflet and shows it to me. "The lawn police are operating in this area" it reads.

'You shouldn't say things like that, Tyler. What if they overhear you and turn up for a midnight inspection,' he says, visibly shaken.

I decide to change the subject. 'How was your day?'

'Busy!' he smiles back.

'Apart from taking selfies of your plants, I mean,' I qualify.

'Oh, in that case not busy,' he says, showing me his phone.

'What about your book?' I ask, feeling worried now.

'Oh I haven't started that yet, I figured I'd settle in first, get the garden up to Happyville standards.'

'My, you use a lot of hashtags,' I say, looking at his timeline.' It feels as though Happyville is changing him too . . . 'Hey Dad, is it all right if the girls and I crash in the den tonight?'

'Yes of course. You kids probably want to get up to mischief, braid each other's hair, talk about boys, and listen to the hit parade on the radio . . . right?'

'Actually, we've got some DNA profiling to crack on with if we're going to solve the long-arm mystery,' I say.

'Oh yes, I see that's all the rage. When I

was young it was sideburns. One day there were no sideburns and then seemingly overnight they were everywhere.'

'Yeah, it's not quite like that, Dad. Enforced spontaneous arm growth and neglecting to shave are pretty different.' Ever since we moved to Happyville, Dad seems happy to ignore that anything strange is going on.

'Well, don't go making any trouble. Folk round here seem to like them, and we don't want to stand out!'

'Yes, I can see how having normal-length arms could cause embarrassment. I'll do my best,' I say, feeling a little annoyed. Dad would never have cared about fitting in before we moved to **HAPPYVILLE**. 'I'm going to the den.

Can you let the girls in when they arrive?'

'No worries, Little Pesca,' Dad smiles, 'it's Italian for "peach",' he adds.

'Yeah, I get it,' I smile. Maybe this dad's still got some life in him yet.

I'm lost in a book about DNA profiling when the door of the trailer swings open, breaking my concentration.

'Hello, I'm here for the sleepover,' Ashley says, bursting in, wearing her PJs and carrying two bags.

'I can't imagine you going to sleep, Ashley. I just assumed you went into standby mode like a computer,' I say, smiling and putting my book down.

'That's a joke isn't it? You're using humour. I read about that somewhere.'

'Were your parents OK with you coming over?'

'Yes, I've given them my number in case there are any problems, but they should be fine. I've left them for the whole night before,' she says, taking a seat.

'What's in the bags? You know it's only one night—we're not going on vacation.'

'This is a humour thing again, isn't it?' she asks. 'The bags contain items from our secret vent in the library and the DNA profiling kit of course.'

'Did someone say sleepover!' Dylan grins,

popping her head round the door. 'I must admit, the thought of spending the whole night with you is a dream come true.'

'Well, thank you Dylan,' I say, surprised.

'I was talking to the computer,' Dylan says, coming into the trailer and stroking her fingers across my computer keyboard.

'Still warm . . .' she says, smelling it as if it were a loaf of freshly baked bread.

'I brought snacks and some bedtime reading!' Dylan opens her backpack and empties thirty to forty bars of candy out on the floor as well as a book on Pythagorus' theorem.

'Ah cool, ancient Greek math!' Ashley cries like an excited kid on Christmas Day.

'Work now, fun later!' I say, grabbing

Ashley's DNA tester from her rucksack.

'HOOK ME UP TO THE MAINFRAME!' Dylan

cries out. Ashley and I look at each other,

puzzled. 'Sorry, I always wanted to say that.'

I grab the DNA profiling kit and plug it into

the computer.

'I'll start analyzing the data,' Ashley says.

'Tyler and I will make a list of all the people

affected so far. We might be able to spot a

pattern,' says Dylan.

'How many more since we've been at

school?' I ask.

'According to the army-like-a-salami

hashtag, at least another fifty,' Dylan says,

looking at her phone, 'If it carries on at this

rate, the whole town will have spaghetti arms

by next week!' she wails.

'Don't worry, we can figure this out and fix it,' I say confidently. 'Dylan, can you get me names and pics of all the victims. I'm going to get some big pens and a large piece of paper to stick to the wall. It isn't a proper investigation until we have a board with pictures and scribbles all over it—I've seen enough crime dramas to know that!'

An hour later and I'm all done. We're sitting back looking at my handiwork while we wait for the DNA results to come through.

'I don't know who these kids are. Can you tell me anything about them?' I turn to Ashley and Dylan.

'Well you already know Blane and

Courtney,' Dylan starts. 'And then there's Carlton—he's in a band and everyone loves him.'

Ashley takes over. 'Then there are the cheerleaders, Tiffany and the other Tiffany— they must have mutated shortly after Courtney did. And then there's another boy called Pip— his dad is rich and so he has lots of friends but he goes to a different school . . .'

'Do they all live near each other?' I ask, but Dylan shakes her head. 'Do they all hang out together? Maybe they caught something from each other?'

Dylan narrows her eyes. 'I doubt it. I mean, some of these people communicate through selfies alone.'

'Huh,' I say. Come on there *must* be a link.
I stare at the photos on the board. I notice they
have all sorts of filters on them, giving them
a faded look, as though they could have been
taken twenty years ago. Still, the filters must be
doing something right, each photo gets loads
of likes.

There is a loud bleep as Ashley's DNA machine finishes its work. She runs over to get the results.

'Could it have something to do with popularity? Social media seems to be the only link . . .' I mutter. Then it hits me like a train. Sometimes the answer is right in front of you.

'That's odd,' Ashley says. The DNA seems to have mutated in a short burst every few days. The last one was—'

'Let me guess, two days ago?'

'Yeah, but how did you . . .?'

'That's when I saw Blane taking a selfie on my first day,' I laugh. 'Look at all the pics. What are they doing?'

'Posing like empty-headed robots,'

Ashley offers.

'Well, yes . . .'

Dylan's hand goes up.

'It's OK, Dylan, you don't have to put your hand up—go ahead.'

'They're selfies. They're all taking selfies!'

'Bingo! The trouble with selfies is that sometimes an—'

'Arm isn't quite long enough?' Ashley interrupts.

'You mean that their arms have suddenly grown so they can take better selfies?' Dylan gasps.

'OH MY! DARRRRRAD!' I shriek.

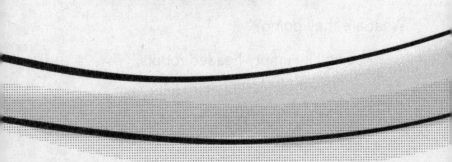

NO SELFIE RESPECT

I rush into the kitchen, Ashley and Dylan behind me. All I can think of is the hundreds of selfies my dad has proudly shown me, of him and his prized plants. They were 'liked' about a million times by Jean!

I burst in to see Dad lifting a huge knife over his head, about to strike down.

'No Dad!' I scream.

'What?' he screams back, 'I'm just cutting

up some bread for supper,' he says, cutting a
long baguette in half.

'I thought you had a long arm! I thought
because you take so many selfies, I thought
you were going to chop it off . . .' I splutter.
I can't help but run over and give him a hug.

'Promise me, no more selfies please!'

'Hey, it's OK,' he says, squeezing me back. 'Anything for my peach. If you're happy, I'm happy. And I see your friends are here—I promise I won't try and be cool in front of them any more either. I noticed how it bothered you the other day.'

'Cool? Wait that's it . . .' I say, looking at the other two. 'It's evolution. They take a pic, post it, it gets lots of likes, and suddenly their brains are full of joy and happiness. They repeat it the next day, and the next, and all it takes is a mutation in the gene pool and suddenly their bodies are growing long arms!'

'But doesn't that take hundreds of years? Giraffes didn't get super-long necks overnight,'

180

Dylan says.

'It's not that crazy actually,' Ashley muses. 'There's a breed of South American lizard, which very suddenly developed sticky feet to climb trees when a new predator was introduced to its jungle environment. It all happened within a few short years.'

'That's what school is though! One big jungle. Everyone trying to compete, and the more popular you are, the better and happier you become.'

'Look!' Dylan says, studying a print out from the DNA machine, 'There's a rush of happiness and a very slight mutation in the arm, and then yesterday at the game the mutation went into overload and Blane's arm just grew and grew.

We've done it, we've solved it!'

We all hold our hands out to do a high five, then remember our previous attempts.

'Actually, let's leave the high five,' I suggest.

'You have to tell someone!' Dad says excitedly. 'I mean, I understood not one word of what you said, but you have to *do* something!'

'Your dad is right. If we don't stop this, what next?' Ashley asks, 'I mean, are we talking big thumbs because of excessive phone use, flapping around like a couple of hot-dog sausages? Is that what we should expect? Maybe ears that become flat like saucers so that big earphones can fit over them. Is this the way the world is going?'

'We need to do something fast!' Dylan snaps.

'I know, we can't live in a world like this!' I agree.

'No, I mean we need to do something before Ashley goes all existential. She can get terribly moody you know,' Dylan whispers to me. And then she turns and says loudly to Ashley, 'Let's put on some lovely jazz, shall we? Which is the one you like? The one that sounds like a piano falling down the stairs?'

Ashley nods and hits the music app on her phone. As the music wafts around her she starts to visibly calm down.

'How are we going to reverse the process?' Dylan asks. She has a good point. I mean, how are we supposed to reverse evolution?

'We need to think outside the box, this isn't a normal physical change and we need to figure out how to jump-start evolution and make it change its mind. But how?' I wonder.

'Well, let's think about this daddy-o,' Ashley adds from her happy jazz place. 'Perhaps we need to do the reverse of what happened?'

'How do you mean?' I ask.

'If taking selfies has suddenly become like a currency to these people, maybe we need to take that away. No more selfies,' Dylan says.

'OK. First thing in the morning, we'll go and talk to Mr Jones—only he has the power to ban selfies from school. He's our only hope,' I say. 'Come on girls, we've got homework to do.'

'Well, it's an interesting theory, girls, but I don't really know what half of those words mean,' Mr Jones says, sitting back in his chair with his feet on the desk, his denim cowboy boots there for all to see. Behind him are a dozen photos of Mr Jones during his modelling days and there's an excruciating amount of denim on display.

'It's simple,' I say, putting away the PowerPoint presentation, printed presentations, 3D model of Blane's DNA strand, and a short animation that we put together last night. 'Stop letting the kids take selfies, otherwise we're all going to end up with giant arms.'

'And that's bad because . . .?' he asks.

'BECAUSE IT'S NOT RIGHT!' I shout, losing my temper. 'Cars will have to be longer so people can actually drive them, we'll all have to buy bigger shirts, people will be able to steal things from around corners, combing your hair will be harder, carrying shopping will be impractical, scratching your head will be impossible. How many reasons do you need? You have to listen to us!'

'But aren't people getting like this because they're popular?' Mr Jones asks, a look of confusion on his face.

'Yes . . .' we all answer.

'Then Happyville High has the most popular students the world!' Mr Jones grins. '**ALL RIIIIIGHT!** Being popular makes you happy, it's written on the school banner, dudettes, I'm surprised you didn't notice that, seeing how you're all so into words.'

Suddenly, Mr Jones starts twitching wildly.

'Great, here goes another one,' I sigh. 'Come on, we're wasting our time.' I gather our materials and we all leave to the sound of '**BOO-YAH!**' coming from Mr Jones' office.

'What now?' Ashley asks.

'I'm scared,' Dylan says.

'It's over.' I just wanted to prove that we could use our brains for good, that we could make a difference to this school. I walk off down the corridor with a heavy heart.

Ashley and Dylan try to follow me but I stop them. 'I just need to be by myself for a while. Maybe I was better off being homeschooled by Dad and then I never would have come to this stupid school. I hoped maybe this time it would be different, but I'm still a nobody who no one listens to.'

'Is she going? Is she leaving us?' Dylan asks Ashley anxiously.

I want to say something to make Dylan feel

better but the truth is, I'm all out of ideas, all out of fight, and I just want to find somewhere quiet so I can be by myself. I open a door, any door, and breathe a sigh of relief to see it's an empty stairwell. I sit on the stairs and get my phone out. I watch as the stock market prices flicker up and down. I really should think about getting in touch with my broker.

I open up my photos—there's one of my old house, my old life. And here is a photo of Mum before she got ill. It's my secret picture, something special just of the two of us. What would *she* do? I wonder. Sometimes I ask her for advice, how stupid is that? I have all the brains in the world and yet I'm the one talking to a photo. I know what she'd say, she'd tell me to stop feeling sorry for myself and she'd tell me not to give up. She could be annoying like that. I allow myself a little grin. It feels harder to remember her the older I get—her face becomes less familiar, but the more time goes by, the more I feel like I really know her. I scroll through my other pictures and there's one of Blane with his long arm, which I had taken when trying to research this ridiculous problem.

'You. Are. Unbelievable!' a voice snarls.

'Courtney!' I say, shutting my phone down quickly.

She grabs me with her long arm and pins me up against the wall. My feet are dangling high above the floor and her face is wild and angry.

'A smile costs nothing,' I say, trying to lighten the mood. 'You don't want people to see you this angry!'

'Yes, but no one can see us, there's no one here but us, Fitz!'

Well it's nice she remembered my name I suppose. Yes she is going to kill me, but at least she knows who she's killing.

'If you are going to do me in, I have some good tips on how to hide a body. I might be able to help,' I blurt out.

'SAY GOODBYE TO YOUR FACE, FREAK!' she snarls, her pouting face foaming at the mouth.

CHAPTER TWELVE

OPERATION LOTS OF WORDS

'SMILE!'

I turn my head to the side to see Dylan and Ashley. At least I think it's them, because they're standing with their backs to me.

Dylan is holding out a phone and suddenly there's a flash and a computerized shutter sound effect.

'What are you doing?' Courtney yells, putting me down. Well, I say putting, more like dropping me on the floor.

'I wanted a selfie with us all, you know, hashtag galpals,' Dylan grins.

'Eh?' Courtney says.

'You seem confused, Courtney, are you OK?' Ashley joins in. 'You've won! It has taken us a while to realize, but your empty, vacuous lifestyle is the future. We don't want to be nerds any more, we want to be like you. We're going to be your friends, we're going to dress like you, walk like you, talk like you, and post selfies of us all together on EVERY social media platform that has ever existed, and we're going to tag you in all of them. Being popular makes you happy, remember!'

'**AAARGH!**' Courtney screams and barges

past Ashley and Dylan, then runs down the corridor.

I rub my neck and when enough time has passed I ask quietly, 'What made you come back?'

'I seem to remember someone telling us that hiding away isn't the right thing to do, and that we need to stand up for ourselves and one another,' Ashley says.

'Nerds stick together!' Dylan grins, before giving me a squeeze.

'So you are still

nerds? You were very convincing when you said that you wanted to be Courtney's friend.'

'I told you we are good actors,' Ashley shrugs. 'Being a nerd is way more fun than being popular.'

'Maybe you're on to something there,' I smile. 'But what are you doing taking selfies? You might get long arms too.'

'Remember that time your dad started talking about music—how did you feel?' Dylan asks.

'Like I never wanted to listen to music again,' I sigh.

'Exactly! When our parents start to take an interest in the music we listen to, suddenly we don't want to listen to it any more, *especially*

when they enjoy it.'

'Are you saying that I should get my dad here to sing at everyone?' I ask, feeling a bit confused.

'No, but who are the uncoolest kids in this school?' Ashley asks.

'Well, us,' I sigh.

Dylan smiles at me encouragingly.

'Wait, are you saying that *we* should start taking selfies?' I ask.

'She's got it!' Ashley chuckles. 'What better way to make the other kids never want to take selfies again, than if a trio of geeks start doing it? We need to not only take selfies, we need to own them. I'm talking selfie the heck out of everything at school.'

'This is perfect! But won't we all get long arms too?' I ask.

'Not according to my calculations. It's a relatively small dose of vanity we're experiencing, we shouldn't suffer any long-term consequences.' Ashley says getting her calculator out.

'Great,' I grin. 'But if we're going to do this, we're going to need to go one step further,' I smile. 'What's the most uncool thing in the world?'

'People trying too hard to be cool?' Ashley suggests.

'Precisely!' I grin. 'We need to try really, really hard to be cool, but first, Phase One . . . to the library!'

'Are you sure this is the best way?' Ashley asks. She's sitting down, blindfolded, in front of her phone. Her fingers are twitching, ready to go.

'**THREE, TWO, ONE, GO!**' I yell, starting the stopwatch. Ashley grabs the phone, figures out which way is up, presses the button on the side, and hits the combination in the keypad using muscle memory.

'The phone is unlocked!' I yell.

'Time?' she asks.

'Five seconds,' I say.

Ashley pauses for a split-second, before pressing the screen. 'I've enabled the camera!' She holds it out in front of her, before angling it just the right amount, and hitting the button on

the side again. There's a loud clicking sound
and she's done.

'Did I get it?' Ashley asks, pulling her
blindfold off and checking the picture. The
snap is good, everything is in focus, and she's
using just the right amount of pout!

'Ashley, you have passed the test,' I grin.

Next, Dylan and I pretend to be walking down the street when . . . what's this we spot? A cute puppy? Actually I don't have a puppy, and since Dylan is allergic to dogs, we're using an old sock instead. Dylan and I stare at each other like a couple of cowboys at high noon. **'DRAW!'** I yell, and quick as a flash we both get our phones out and take selfies of ourselves and the cute sock . . . I mean puppy. We are a precision team, primed and loaded.

'We are almost ready,' I announce. 'Now for Phase Two.'

I grab the fashion homework-book out of my bag. 'Who knew this would come in useful?' I say, flicking through the pages. 'Let's take our inspiration for trying too hard to look cool from here,' I say. 'Then everyone meet in the library first thing tomorrow morning for "Operation Let's Pretend to be Cool So We Can make selfies totally uncool and Stop People's Arms Growing Really Big!"'

'I must say,' Ashley says the next morning, pulling some twigs out of her hair, 'that when we agreed to be friends, I didn't realize there'd be so much dressing up involved.'

'What's happened to your hair?' I ask.

'Oh, I popped home to get some stuff and it turns out giving seven cats coffee is a very bad idea. I don't suppose you have a tetanus shot going spare do you?'

'Sorry, no.' I shake my head, 'sorry about all the disguises,' I say. 'I must admit I didn't really expect it either . . . Still, I think it's been fun. Anyway, let's see what we've got.' We spill the contents of our bags on the floor. There's a red lipstick, a couple of wigs, some hairspray, frilly, patterned blouses, as well as baseball caps and all manner of other accessories. I look at Ashley and Dylan.

'We did our best,' Dylan shrugs.

'This is perfect! We will look absolutely ridiculous.'

'I did some googling and apparently the hipster or cool thing to do, is to mismatch everything as well as use things from the past. Also, beards are very popular,' Ashley says, pulling up some pictures on her phone.

'Hmmm,' says Dylan, stroking her chin. 'This is just what we need.'

Ten minutes later, we're finished and ready to go. I'm wearing a pair of flared trousers that Dylan's mum used to wear whenever she went to the discotheque, along with a big blonde wig, sunglasses, and wedged boots that may as well be stilts. I totter around like a horse on tiptoes. 'How do I look?' I ask the other two.

'Ridiculous,' they both answer.

'Perfect!' I grin.

Dylan is wearing a baseball cap backwards, which she's teamed with her dad's old shirt, also from the discotheque era, that she's matched with a pair of sports shorts, knee-length socks, and roller skates.

'I'm not sure about the beard,' I say, wrinkling my nose.

'Ashley said beards are hip right now, so I drew one on with this make-up pen—do I look like Charles Darwin?' Dylan asks hopefully.

I haven't the heart to tell her that she's used a permanent Sharpie pen.

'I like it,' she says. 'May even keep it for a while.'

'Well, you may have to,' I mutter.

I look at Ashley, who's wearing wellington boots, along with a summer dress and arm bands, the sort you might wear to the pool if you're not a confident swimmer.

'What–what–' Ashley stutters, looking down at herself. 'What if we're so cool that we actually make selfies even cooler than they are already?'

'Oh my, I didn't think of that!' Dylan looks horrified.

'I think . . . I think we'll be OK. We look like a garage sale just chewed us up and spat us out. We need to try and sound cool though. I mean, if we're just ourselves, they won't take us seriously,' I add.

'Oh, I know!' Dylan says, putting her hand up. 'We should just say "like" a lot. They always say "like", like totally loads. Oh, and "totally" too.'

'Good tip!' I say. 'Anything else?'

'Use nouns as verbs,' Ashley says. 'Instagram me later, Snapchat me up sometime. That sort of thing.'

'Again, good tip. And did you both manage to sign up to every social media outlet that's humanly possible?'

Both girls nod.

'Good. Then we're ready. We need to work ourselves into the groups of normals and selfie everything. I'm talking photobombing if necessary. Now have we all been practising our pouty faces?' I ask. We all take turns doing them.

'Great, we look like a load of angry fish. This is, like, totally perfect! Now let's hashtag the heck out of this town!'

'Hey, everyone, I'm Tyler, Tyler Fitz, and I thought it would be really cool if we could totally like get a selfie, with everyone, you know, it's like totally a really cool school and I love my new friends, so who wants in?' I yell out in the middle of the schoolyard. Everyone turns and stares at me.

'Don't be fooled by the sunglasses that I've got, I'm still Tyler from the block, here to keep it hashtag real.' I cross my two fingers from each hand to make a hashtag (I should probably copyright that, I could make a fortune). I look around as everyone looks back at me in horror. I pull out my phone and Dylan and Ashley spend an inordinate amount of time fluffing up their hair, making sure Ashley's arm bands are pumped up enough, and that Dylan's beard hasn't rubbed off by accident (no danger there), before we finally pull our angry fish faces and snap.

'I'll tag you Tiffany the Second!' I gleefully shout. 'Has anyone seen Blane? I want to get a picture of him for my blog.'

There is a murmuring at the school gates as people start to put their phones away and head to their classes. So far so good. Ashley and I lock our scooters up and head inside.

'There's Courtney,' Ashley says. 'And she looks annoyed.'

'You!' Courtney comes over, big arm first of course!

SNAP!

Ashley takes a quick selfie with her.

'Love!' I say.

'No, no, no! I didn't say you could take a

selfie with me! What makes you think I want to be in your picture?'

I notice the Tiffanies are gathering behind Courtney but I don't let it deter me. 'I love what you've done with your hair, what do you call that?' I say in a sickly-sweet voice as though we're best friends.

'I combed it, you should try it sometime,' she huffs. 'What on earth are you wearing? Is this a joke? Is this Halloween? Why are you dressed like a dork, or rather, even more dorky than usual I mean?'

'Oh, you're so funny!' Ashley says, smiling. I don't think I've seen Ashley smile before. It looks so false and odd, it's perfect.

'I think we should totally throw Courtney

a party,' Ashley continues. 'She can invite the Tiffanies, eat popcorn, watch music videos, and talk about boys, like Blane. He's a boy, isn't he? Hashtag best friends for ever!'

'We are not friends!' Courtney says, getting more and more angry.

SNAP! I take another quick selfie.

'Will you stop doing that?' Tiffany One says.

'So sorry, we can't help our selfies!' Dylan grins. 'Don't worry, we'll tag you on all the social media platforms, all of them, every single one of them including Google Plus, which no one uses any more.'

'Please don't! Look, I'm giving all the money I ever took from you back, see?' she says, hitting her phone.

'Too late, I've just like totally Instagrammed it. Look, I've used a really cool filter, it makes the picture look like a rubbish one from thirty years ago, isn't technology great!' I squeal. I've noticed that squealing is very much the done thing.

'I'm going to get Blane,' Courtney says. 'He'll sort you out.'

'Oh, I love Blane, hashtag secret stalker love!' I say.

'We can all have a picture together and then we can create a WhatsApp group and like chat to each other all the time and we can all hang out and probably like all stay in touch for the rest of our lives. I love you Courtney, I love everything about you.' **SNAP!** 'Can you show me how you do your hair and teeth? I love the way you wear your teeth, right out there so everyone can see them.'

'**LEAVE ME ALONE!**' Courtney says, running away. 'You freaks aren't like us, why are you trying to be like us? You belong in the library. Stop being us!'

As Courtney runs, her arm begins to twitch like a snake being electrocuted.

'Look!' Ashley says. 'It's working, it's

beginning to shrink!' We stare as Courtney's arm gets smaller by a few inches.

'This is brilliant!' I cry. 'We need to spread out, that way we can annoy way more people.'

We spend the rest of the morning taking as many pictures as we can, posting them as often as we can, and letting everyone know that we've posted them. Dylan does some top work taking pictures with the teachers, who it seems are even more uncool than us. Ashley decides to live-blog the whole thing, which she sends out to everyone via the in-school computer system.

By lunchtime we have made selfies and social media the most unpopular thing in Happyville High. We all sit down for lunch to compare notes, once we've all taken pictures with our lunch of course.

'So far so good. How are people's arms doing?' I ask.

Ashley gets out her phone. 'People have stopped posting stuff, so it's hard to tell, but—'

Just then, there's a huge cry from across the other side of the cafeteria. A boy with a long arm begins to jibber and yell, '**BOO-YAH**!' at the top of his voice before his arm shoots straight up in the air. We all stare. What's going to happen? Will it grow even longer and punch through the roof? No, it shrinks! The boy laughs like it's tickling as it shrinks down to normal size. It worked, it actually worked. We did it!

'You see, I knew it would work!' Ashley

giggles with excitement.

'We are so uncool that, merely by being *this* unpopular, we have reversed evolution. Now that is ultimate power!' Dylan grins.

Just at that second, Blane comes into the cafeteria and storms over to us.

'Courtney told me what you did; that you took her picture and you posted it online, without checking if she was happy with her hair or anything—what kind of monster are you?'

SNAP! I take another quick picture.

'Will you stop that? I know what you've been up to, I know you're trying to be normal like us, but you're not allowed to be normal!'

'Says the boy with an arm like a giant bratwurst,' I say, shaking my head.

'What is it you want?' he sneers.

'How can you be angry? I just want to be like you. You don't like us being different, so we're going to be the same as you. We're all going to be like each other. I see that you and Courtney were right; we don't want to be freaks any more. Being popular makes you happy, REMEMBER! So what better way to do that than by trying a few selfies,' I grin.

'Come on, Blane, just take one selfie with us. You know you want to, you know selfies are your favourite, just a quick one,' Dylan says, holding up her phone.

'NO. I DON'T WANT TO DO ANY MORE SELFIES EVER AGAIN! WE'RE NOT THE SAME. YOU WILL NEVER BE POPULAR. STOP.

STOP TRYING TO BE LIKE US AND STOP BEING IN LOVE WITH ME, IT'S HORRIBLE! I CAN'T TAKE IT ANY MORE!!!' Blane screams, before twitching and lassoing his arm around his head. He falls to the floor and with a sad yell of '**BOO-YAH!**' he throws his arm in the air and it shrinks, all the way down to normal-size again.

Our work here is done.

The rest of the day sees all the armies-like-salamis go back to normal size again. We stroll out of school feeling very happy with ourselves.

'There's Blane coming out of the coach's office, he looks terrible,' says Ashley.

'Please coach, just because my arm's small again doesn't mean I can't be quarterback.

Who else are you going to put in the team anyway? I'm the best!' he pleads.

Courtney has her arm around him and shoots me a filthy look. I smile back.

'You know what? We make a pretty good team,' Dylan says.

'We do,' Ashley agrees. 'This place is pretty strange you know, but I think between the three of us there's nothing we can't handle.'

'Hey look, it's those girls who saved everyone's arms!' I hear a kid call out from behind me. We all turn around, smiling triumphantly.

'Now I can't take really rad selfies any more!' And he barges into us as though we're skittles in a bowling alley.

'Ouch! Hello? I'm standing right here. You are welcome by the way!' I yell after him. I turn to Dylan and Ashley, 'Well so much for people being grateful. Perhaps Happyville High doesn't want us, but they may well need us. I mean, if people's arms can mutate overnight, who knows what might happen next? We've got the brains, and we've got the den as our HQ. Being popular sure isn't everything, so what do you say to calling ourselves the Misfits of Happyville?' I hold up my hand, and for once we do it—we all manage to do a high-five without smacking each other in the face.

'**TO THE MISFITS!**' we all yell.

It's a perfect way to spend a very odd week. I'm so pleased I made it through, we all did.

'Back to mine for some boiled rice and pop tarts?' I ask.

Scooting through town we see people's arms recoiling like slinkies back to their normal size.

'Hey, I'm looking forward to getting out of these clothes,' I say.

'Me too. No more disguises, no more dressing up!' Ashley agrees.

As we scoot up to my house, Dad meets us at the front gate. I smile and wave.

'Good day at school?' he asks.

'The best,' I say. 'Do you mind if the girls stay for dinner?'

'Sure. Your day is about to get even better,' he grins. 'I'll fix you something healthy, you'll need it.'

'Why?' we all ask.

'I just had the coach on the phone. All three of you have made the football team!'

#selfietime

#harderthanitlooks

#ilovemybeard!

#bffselfie

#where'smyface

#where'smyface

#shoegoals

#nerdsrule

LOOK OUT FOR MORE

HAPPYVILLE HIGH

COMING SOON!

ABOUT THE AUTHOR

Before becoming a writer and illustrator Tom
spent nine years working as political cartoonist
for *The Western Morning News* thinking up
silly jokes about even sillier politicians. Then, in
2004 Tom took the plunge into illustrating and
writing his own books. Since then he has written
and illustrated picture books and fiction as well
as working on animated TV shows for Disney and
Cartoon Network.

Tom lives in Devon and his hobbies include
drinking tea, looking out of the window, and
biscuits. His hates include spiders and running
out of tea and biscuits.

OTHER BOOKS BY

Tom McLaughlin

THE Accidental
PRESIDENT

FIRST KID PRESIDENT!

1

Tom McLaughlin

THE Accidental
PRIME MINISTER

'HATS FOR CATS!'

10

Tom McLaughlin

THE Accidental
FATHER CHRISTMAS

IT'S A CRACKER!

Tom McLaughlin

Ready for more great stories?

Try one of these ...

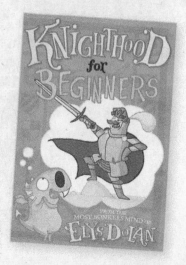